Malunkyaputta
His Quest for Edification

by
Cornel Adam

Dragon's Teeth Press
2015

Printed in the United States of America.

ISBN 978-0-934218-14-6

Dragon's Teeth Press
Georgetown, California
Shaw Island, Washington
dragons-teeth-press.com

Special thanks to Theo Lengyel for scanning the manuscript
and to Sebastian Lengyel for photographs of Cornel.

Contents

"... Bear always in mind what it is that I have not explained and what it is that I have explained... And what *have* I explained, Malunkyaputta? Misery have I explained: the origin of misery, the cessation of misery, and the path leading to the cessation of misery have I explained."

– Buddha, the Awakened One

Prologue: The Quibbler

In his earlier life Malunkyaputta had been a disciple of Buddha the Awakened One. He sat at the master's feet in the deer park by the Ganges and heard the master's lessons in company of other would-be gurus. But while his fellow students listened quietly or hummed the holy word *Om*, Malunkyaputta was always asking questions. A thin dark youth with bright eyes and a skeptical smile, he was seldom satisfied with Buddha's answers.

"I crave to be edified," he would interrupt the master's lectures. "I want to know the first and final facts. What is my most important study? Where should I start? Why and when?"

"Start with alpha, skip to omega, omit the abracadabra and follow the twelve rules," Buddha would tell him patiently. "The more a fool hears the less he understands. The more he questions the less he learns. The more he knows the more he forgets."

"I crave to know all!" cried Malunkyaputta.

Buddha smiled distantly. "I taught you the Four Noble Truths," he repeated. "I taught you the eight-fold way: right thoughts, right speed, right acts, and so forth. I taught you the cause and cure of human suffering. I taught you that desire is the chief cause of suffering." (By desire he meant lust for copulation.) "Desire breeds poverty, hunger, overcrowding, war, disease, and death. I taught you to overcome desire. I taught you the right way to Nirvana."

"I need more edification," said Malunkyaputta. "What exactly do you mean by the *right* way to Nirvana?" Rather than overcoming his desires, Malunkyaputta hoped to fulfill them and thereby attain a state of happiness.

Buddha sighed wearily. He understood Malunkyaputta the way he understood theologians who enjoyed arguing about how many angels could dance on the point of a pin. Buddha himself was an atheist. He had tried to reform the old religion with its many gods and superstitious priests.

"Be a lamp unto yourself," he told Malunkyaputta, dismissing him. "Go your own way. You are excused."

1

Observing the master's rejection of his youngest disciple, his fellow students were quick to turn on Malunkyaputta. They jeered at him and called him names. Padman-Ananda in particular, his chief rival, taunted him. A short deep-chested fellow with penetrating eyes, Padman-Ananda implied that Malunkyaputta was the offspring of untouchables. His ancestors were chimpanzees from Madagascar or bushmen from Africa or Jews from the court of King Solomon who, searching for a new trade route, had been shipwrecked off the coast of India. According to Padman-Ananda, the rejected disciple was closely related to a chimp, a nigger, or a Jew. In truth, Malunkyaputta was made from the mingled dust of the earth and the stars. Every cell in his body testified to the fact that he was linked to every form of life, both plant and animal, reaching back to the first blob of protoplasm that appeared on the face of a sun-washed rock by a steaming sea. As a matter of fact, Padman-Ananda and Malunkyaputta resembled each other; they resembled a million other Hindu students, from the days of Buddha to the days of Radhakrishnan and Aurobindo; all were afflicted with a hunger for spiritual light and a craving for the transcendental.

The apprentice gurus pelted Malunkyaputta. They flung rotten-ripe figs into the quibbler's face. They tossed banana peels on his head. They threw cow dung on his white dhoti. They chased him from the deer park. Then they danced back to their master in the shade of the bodhi tree to resume their study of the right way to Enlightenment through meditation, mindfulness, compassion and lovingkindness. The would-be lamas and swamis hoped to become future buddhas or bodhi-sattvas. They hummed the holy word *Aum*, and chanted their sacred syllables:

"Mantra, tantra, dharma, karma...
Sutra-deva, dona-soma...
Bodhi-citta, citta-mani...
Tantra, mantra, karma, dharma..."

Malunkyaputta shook the cow dung from his tunic. He wiped the dirt from his head and face. Fixing his eyes on the invisible stars, he silently affirmed his secret aspirations. "I will find new wisdom," he told himself, "fresh as the world's first dawn, sharp as a thorn, true and enduring as the stars. I will discover new beauty to match the spring. I will invent a new poem, sweet as wild honey, strong as a lion's heart. And I will win the world's esteem..."

So Malunkyaputta embarked on his quest for edification.

No one knew his mother or father. Abandoned as an infant, he was found one day floating down the Ganges in a tangle of weeds and garbage, like baby Moses in the basket of bulrushes. An old woman walking along the riverside as if in search of something heard the infant crying. She drew him out of the water, a never-ending tide of corpses and abortions. She saved him, adopted him, and gave him the name Malunkyaputta, whose meaning she alone knew.

Capricious in temper, she was both kind and cruel, punishing or rewarding him according to her unpredictable moods. At times, she seemed rich and selfish; at times, poor and generous. She had traveled far and wide and understood many strange things. At one time she had been in charge of the crematorium in Bangladesh. When Malunkyaputta was able to speak, she taught him to call her Our Precious Lady Stepmother. (Later he called her Marah, which means "bitter".)

When he was six years old she sent him to a charity school in Bombay. Here he learned Sanskrit and began to study the Vedas. In time, he learned the great Hindu myths of creation, the birth of order from Chaos, the origin of good and evil, the works of gods and demons. He learned a thousand sacred hymns, the rites of Indra, Mithra, Agni, and Soma; legends of the lost mothers Tiamat and Veritra, the Serpent-Father and the river-goddess Sarasvati. Later he learned about reincarnation and the cycles of rebirth and suffering... He later studied other scriptures: the Bible, the Gnostic Gospels, the Kabbalah, but became increasingly skeptical. At 18, he joined the ashram of Buddha the Awakened One, hoping to become properly edified.

* * *

His questions had provoked his expulsion from the deer park. To understand the true reasons for man's recurrent unhappiness, he felt he needed more experience in the world of his fellowmen. The world of nature itself seemed to him beautiful. The galaxies unfolding overhead and around the Earth resembled a miraculous efflorescence of light, flowering for billions of years. In comparison with eternity, their life was brief of course, as brief as the bloom of a melon flower. Yet he had time enough for his season, time enough to ask his first and last questions. And he asked himself: "If I with my eroding eyes may behold the flowering stars and, with my perishable lungs, may breathe the immortal air, why should I not be able to understand the true meaning of life? Or understand myself, with the monkeys dancing inside me, performing their tricks and asking so many first and last questions?"

After his expulsion, he returned to Bombay, a big city more crowded than before. To become what he hoped to become, he intended to emulate the best philosophers. He would test their lessons, avoid their mistakes, and adapt to his own purpose whatever seemed practical.

Imitating young Buddha's example, he dressed himself in a mendicant's tattered yellow robe and took up his station on a busy corner near the docks. His Precious Lady Stepmother gave him a begging bowl. "This bowl has a special virtue," she remarked with a cryptic smile. "It can never be filled..." (Later she supplied him with a passport, a credit card, and a small round shaving mirror. "This may help you to recognize yourself," she said.)

So begging for alms and chanting his mantras, Malunkyaputta observed with his own eyes the seemingly real world of his long-suffering fellowmen. He watched the crowds in the street: an endless procession of the poor, the hungry, the homeless; the lame, the halt, and the blind. He saw demented dreamers, pleasure-seekers and parasites. He saw laborers from the rice fields, fruit vendors, stevedores; merchants, lawyers, students, clerks; holy men, thieves and murderers, lepers and untouchables, young and old—all in bondage to their myths and superstitions. Some tossed him a small coin or a crust of bread. Others shrugged or turned away from him in contempt. Each passerby was a separate world; each was a solitary cell, burdened with fears and loneliness. Each seemed to be mutely asking himself thorny old questions: "Who am I?...What's happening to me?... What's the meaning of it all?..."

After observing the scene for a while, Malunkyaputta began to see the obvious. As Buddha had already remarked, the mass of people were afflicted with ignorance, disease, desire, vanity, greed, boredom, old age, and death. Suffering was widely distributed; delusion was rampant; compassion, scarce; understanding, elusive. "How may I help them?" Malunkyaputta asked himself. The crowds of the poor and demented never seemed to diminish. "How can I entertain them?" The people, absorbed in themselves, ignored his mantras. "I may need more edification..." To cheer himself, he invented a new mantra. "If you cannot amuse the poor people, try to annoy them. If you cannot annoy them, try to amuse yourself."

4

In the spring of the year, Bombay held a festival in honor of Brahma, Vishnu, and Shiva, the Hindu trinity of androgynous gods who, mingling in men's affairs, could assume all sorts of masks and disguises. They symbolized the Creator, the Preserver and the Destroyer. Malunkyaputta witnessed the celebration from his station by the docks. He watched a line of graceful dancers and actors in traditional costumes; acrobats, tumblers, jugglers; magicians, rope-climbers, fire-eaters, and snake charmers with cobras. He heard bands of musicians beating their drums and gongs and cymbals. He heard ecstatic flute players improvising mystical music in minor keys with endless variations. The conductor of the musicians resembled Padman, his rival in the ashram. Padman passed by with a glance of contempt at the poor quibbler.

The procession was followed by a splendid coach-and-four which carried a beautiful and solitary young woman, richly gowned. Was it Mia? A royal visitor from a palace in Kashmir? A sacred whore from the temple in Benares? A goddess in disguise? Mia held a bouquet of blue lotus in her arms. When her coach passed by the handsome young mendicant, she smiled at him and tossed him the bouquet. She seemed infinitely beautiful and infinitely desirable. He longed to cast a spell over her. He wanted to know her, body and soul, but didn't know how to approach her. He felt profoundly ignorant. Beauty was as difficult and elusive as wisdom.

* * *

Pursuing his quest for edification, Malunkyaputta made a long hard trek to Tibet. In the shadow of the magnificent Himalayas, he found the lamasery in Lhasa, the seat of the Dalai Lama. The Lama and his disciples welcomed the young pilgrim. After his death-defying trek, they considered him a promising recruit to their order.

Before long, they taught him their occult arts and shared their traditional stock-in-trade: telepathy, clairvoyance, crystal reading, recalling past lives, predicting the future. Within a few months, Malunkyaputta learned the yogis' way of transcendental meditation; their rules of self-realization and self-overcoming; their doctrines of reincarnation and transmigration. He learned the true date of his birth and death, and the date of his next incarnation. He learned to alter his states of consciousness. He learned the techniques of deep sleep, voluntary dreaming, suspended animation, self-hypnosis. He took part in their love feasts in which they celebrated their fellowship by sampling each other's turds. He could walk on water or sleep on beds of fire. He became adept in composing koans or riddles without an answer. If he wished, he could speak in tongues—including Greek, Hebrew, German, and Gibberish—and handle snakes as well.

By drawing on his mind power, Malunkyaputta could exercise his gift of imagination. He now used it to teach himself levitation. By applying the *Als Ob* or "As If" principle, he could realize to objects of his fantasy and acquire new means of locomotion. Levitation enabled him to overcome his time-space limitations. It furnished him with an inexpensive way of traveling. It allowed him to transcend the three dimensions of space and the fourth dimension of time. No longer bound by time or space, he could go wherever he wished. Like Ezekiel he could levitate over valleys of bones; like Dante he could visit his neighbors in diverse circles of hell or heaven. He could pursue his edification without the restrictions of time, place, history or geography. He could interview the great seers of all times and places.

Using his poet's license, he left the lamasery and levitated over the vast plains and valleys and holy places of India: Bankura, Kathmandu, Madras, and many more. He levitated across the steppes of Mongolia and the Gobi Desert until he reached the Province of Lu where he visited Confucius.

The sage of China had composed a Book of Songs, a Book of Music, a Book of Rites and Rituals. He had devised a thousand rules for reforming the people and their rulers. He taught respect for one's ancestors, whoever they may be. After listening to Malunkyaputta's rambling story of his quest for edification, Confucius told him: "Alas, my friend, you may be one of the unteachable. You use so many words I cannot understand your meaning. If you wish to consult me, please rectify your speech. Use the simplest words to say exactly what you mean. If you cannot say what you mean, please practice the art of silence."

Malunkyaputta thanked the sage of China and went to interview Lao-Tse, a neighbor of Confucius. Lao-Tse lived like a hermit in the woods and did not care for reformers. "Rest easy, my friend," he told his visitor. "A mountain bears great forests on its back and makes no noise about it...The man who knows keeps silent. The man who doesn't know may talk too much."

Malunkyaputta then levitated southward to consult with Zarathustra. "God is ailing," the Persian told him. "He needs man's help against satan. Your task is to choose. Choose to help God or Satan in the powers of light or the powers of darkness."

He visited the Near East where Moses advised him: "Keep the Ten Commandments, and you'll never go wrong..." Jesus reduced the ten to two and told Malunkyaputta: "If you're an atheist, you need observe only one. The most important rule is: Love your neighbor as yourself." "But that's the hardest commandment," said Malunkyaputta. "Who could learn to follow it?" "Then love yourself as your neighbor," said Jesus. "Is that any easier?"

Mohammed advised him: "Study the Koran. It's better than the Vedas or the Bible. Believe me, young man, I am the greatest prophet, greater than Moses or Jesus! The Koran has all the answers... Great is Allah and Mohammed is his Prophet!"

Swinging through time-space, Malunkyaputta consulted several venerable poets. Gilgamesh in Sumeria told him of his search for the tree of immortality. He visited blind Homer and his school of bards by the wine-dark Aegean Sea and heard him recite the adventures of Ulysses after the ruinous war with Troy... He interviewed Pindar who had won many Olympic prizes for his odes. The Greeks honored their poets as much as their athletes, and their poets sought to be master teachers of the people. (Incidentally, anyone may consult dead sages or poets, even without the aid of levitation: Whether on clay tablets, parchment scrolls or microfilm, a dead poet's surviving words may speak to the inquisitive anywhere.)

He visited Aristophanes who laughed at the quester incredulously and snorted: "Brrk-kek-kek!" He called on Lucretius who told him: "Atoms! We're nothing but atoms in random collision! I explained it all by the light of Democritus! Look and be wise and be gone!" He looked up Virgil who said: "I followed my master Homer. A better magician..." He consulted Shakespeare who smiled at him curiously, as he might have smiled on Caliban, and told him: "Look in your mirror, as I did, and hold your mirror up to Nature..." He consulted Dante, Milton, Kalidasa. The great poets gazed at him distantly and shook their heads. They had revealed their open secrets in thousands of luminous lines, in Purgatorio, Paradise Lost, Sakuntala, yet few understood their parables.

In Athens, Malunkyaputta visited Socrates and solicited his advice. "Know your self," said Socrates. "The unexamined life is not worth living. I myself claim to know nothing." How does a Greek become wise? Malunkyaputta wondered. By claiming to know nothing... How may I become wise? By imitating Socrates... Socrates himself had quizzed the best poets in Athens but found that none of them could explain his methods. The poets seemed to compose their revelations in fits of madness or in a state of irrational frenzy. Yet they considered themselves authorities on all things under the sun. Aristophanes had lampooned Socrates as a sophist.

Malunkyaputta interviewed Plato in his Academy, a garden-like school on the outskirts of the city. Plato recounted his Parable of the Cave. "You too are a prisoner in that cave," he told Malunkyaputta. "You too are deceived by shadows which you take for the real world...The shadows you pursue are illusions. They are but blurred and faulty imitations of the Good, the True, and the Beautiful. The originals dwell in the realm of immortal ideas..." A poet himself, Plato wanted to banish poets from his utopia, depicting the scandalous lives of the gods, poets were a source of moral confusion.

Malunkyaputta consulted Aristotle. Plato's best student, Aristotle was more of a scientist than a philosopher. He regarded Plato as a mystic rather than a thinker. "Man is the most inquisitive and most imitative animal," he told Malunkyaputta. "His capacity to reason sets him apart from the beasts..." He referred Malunkyaputta to his works which summarized all the best knowledge of his times.

* * *

He pondered the wisdom of the seers and sages. The great men of the past offered glimpses of the truth. Some furnished brilliant flashes of insight and illumination. Others weighed the most difficult problems and drew durable conclusions. Still others told what could be told in terms as clear and simple as anyone could hope. Who could better explain the meaning of man or unravel the enfolding mystery of things? Who could improve the art of Homer or Shakespeare? Who could argue with Socrates? Who could penetrate farther than Plato or Aristotle?

Yet Malunkyaputta wasn't satisfied. He still had too many questions which needed answering. He craved an ultimate truth which he hadn't yet found. Was this his karma? To drift in a cloud of doubt and uncertainty, despite his high conjectures and all his borrowed knowledge?

He returned to his gurus in Tibet. The lamas were displeased with his metaphysical questions. They condemned his experiments in interviewing the dead. They considered him in bondage to dangerous illusions. When Malunkyaputta tried to justify his own way of pursuing the truth, they resolved to dismiss him from the brotherhood. They purged from his memory the occult arts they had taught him. They revoked his poet's license to levitate. They restored him to his original ignorance. Then, chanting appropriate mantras of malediction, they drove him out of the lamasery.

Malunkyaputta stumbled through the awesome wastelands of the snow-covered Himalayas. He lost himself in the cold white wilderness. Sliding down an endless slope, he fell from a high ledge into an icy abyss. His last thought while falling was: "Alas! Is this my fate? To pass from the world unedified?"

He fell on a slab of rock at the edge of a crevice. The Himalayas towered over him and pressed on him like immovable glaciers. Soon he was frozen solid. Bereft of breath, he was technically dead. Bereft of all signs of life, he was virtually dead. He was in fact completely dead.

This ought to mark the end of our story. But those who might welcome our sorry hero's exit may have forgotten Homer's practical invention: *Deus ex machina.*

Three familiar figures, robed like Tibetan leopard hunters, stood in the snow on the ledge of rock and gazed meditatively at the frozen body. Malunkyaputta lay on the rock like the cadaver of a goat or a leopard.

"The quibbler mocked the Buddha," said Padman-Ananda. "He questioned the truth…"

"He derided his teacher," said Our Precious Lady Stepmother.

"He pursued the path of illusion," said Mia.

The three turned toward each other speculatively.

"Who can teach the unteachable?"

"Should he escape to Nirvana or be born again?"

"Should we end our experiment?"

They turned again and came to a decision:

"Let him suffer the Wheel again…"

"Let him know his karma."

"Let him be edified."

They hummed their mysterious syllables: "Mantra, tantra, dharma, karma," and Malunkyaputta stirred as if preparing for a rebirth. A part of him suspected that the godlike figures in front of him were projections of his fantasy or fragments from his dream time, drawn from his unconscious.

Dreaming that he was dead, frozen in the ice of the Himalayas, Malunkyaputta remained suspended in time and space for more than twenty-five centuries.

Then he suffered a rebirth in accordance with his karma.

*   *   *

Malunkyaputta appeared in London as a visiting student from Bombay on the first of April in the middle of the 20th century. If you doubt the theory of reincarnation, you may find this incredible. Yet is it much more incredible than the plain fact that you were born at a particular time and place, whether in London, Bombay, Kamchatka or Chattanooga, and that you are reading these lines at a particular time and place? As for reincarnation, many believe in resurrection. May we not suppose that, in a sense, each day when we wake from sleep, we suffer a kind of resurrection?

Part One

Noon Song

Noon so clear
     night so long,
Shall I not dare
     invent a song?

Time so little
     change so near,
Words so brittle,
     who will hear?

Let him who can
     turn air to song:
Breath in man
     lasts not long.

Chapter I. The Student

In pursuit of edification, Malunkyaputta audited some of the best schools in both the Old World and the New. He heard scholars at Cambridge, Oxford, the Sorbonne; Prague, Vienna, Salamanca; Heidelberg, Nuremberg, Berlin, Buchenwald; he also heard advanced thinkers at Harvard, Princeton, Yale, Cornell, M.I.T. Between 1950 and 1960 he heard the new physicists explain the universe from the First Big Bang which occurred some fifteen billion years ago to the Grand Unifying Theory which would combine the laws of physics in the mind of God within the next fifteen billion years or so. They spoke of crowded space: of an ever-expanding world; of black holes which swallowed up galaxies; of the Last Big Bang which would end the show.

He heard other scholars explain the more immediate scene. A follower of Reverend Malthus observed: "The poor are breeding too fast, as always. The Earth cannot feed them all. Too many people, not enough food. Nature must reduce them, by famine, plague, or war. As always…" A disciple of Darwin explained: "Life improves by selection. Nature eliminates the weak, only the fittest deserve to survive. Only the fittest deserve the gift of life…"

He learned that in addition to murdering several million Jews, the Germans had sought to purge the Third Reich of some 70,000 Gypsies. A proud, fatalistic, brown-skinned people, who may have migrated from India, the Gypsies were outcasts who preserved their Romany songs and dances and strange tribal lore. Malunkyaputta felt a bond with the persecuted Gypsies, many of whom were incinerated in Auschwitz.

A student of Himmler declared: "Aryans are the master race. Our mission is to purge the Earth of its defectives."

The Leader himself had left his own legacy:

Trapped below the rubble of my realm,
betrayed by a deluded rabble,
I call on my heirs to redeem my vision.
Hear me, my sons to come! I leave you my works;
my maps to Valhalla, my blueprints for the future.

I leave you my master plan: to breed a new race of heroes,
to rule the earth for a thousand years,
and bury the deceitful tribe of Jews for ever!
These words are my dragon's teeth. My heirs shall not fail.
More numerous than the bones in the burning pits,
my death-eyed sons shall rise from the earth and prevail!

Malunkyaputta heard post-modern philosophers who followed Wittgenstein explain: "Philosophy is but a game of words. It has no particular meaning…" Elsewhere, Professors Muddler, Haydigger, Derider, and Driveler amused themselves by multiplying words to deconstruct Aristotle, Descartes, Kant, with other less sophisticated speculators. He heard military historians explain how and why civilized Europeans killed 100 million of their fellowmen in two world wars at the behest of their leaders. One historian described the twentieth century as the most horrible age in the annals of mankind. Another called it The Age of Stupifying Progress.

He visited museums and galleries from the Prado to the Hermitage and the caves of Altamira. He studied the images of man from Neanderthal to post-Picasso. He went to film archives and saw documentary films which showed the life of 20th century man as graphically as the pictures carved on the walls of Thebes and Karnak showed the life of the Egyptians in the 20th century B.C. The moving pictures he saw in the archives gave him candid views of modern people preparing to make war. He watched the grand rallies, the sea of flags and banners, the torchlight parades. He heard the eloquent speeches that turned the multitudes into huge armies with guns and tanks and planes; seething with resentment, thirsty for revenge, hungry for glory and lebensraum. He studied the features of the people's leaders, in Germany, Italy, Russia: Mussolini, Hitler, Stalin. All of them were dead already. Il Duce, strung up by his heels in Milan; Der Fuehrer, burrowed in his bunker in Berlin; Stalin, poisoned by his doctors in Moscow. Already, their once-terrifying images were fading from the screen, to merge with the ghostly company of earlier earth-shakers and death-makers: Sennacherib, Sardanapalus, Genghis Khan. He watched the opening up of the torture camps, with their surviving remnant of slaves and living cadavers.

He witnessed the trials at Nuremberg: victors and victims, survivors or losers, the spectacle was part of a receding past. The same year of the trials was marked by the dropping of the bomb over Hiroshima, and the unveiling shadow of the mushroom shaped cloud now loomed over mankind.

A visiting lecturer at Buchenwald University treated the past as a flexible text, subject to revision in accord with the historian's capacity for invention. The techniques developed in Auschwitz, for example, utilizing gas chambers and Zyklon-B, were in effect a branch of Sanitary Engineering applied to surplus population. In some cases, the lecturer explained, genocide was perhaps the right solution.

Emulating Socrates, Malunkyaputta questioned the pretensions of the experts.

"I crave to be edified," he said. "What exactly do you mean by the *right* solution?" He was ejected from Buchenwald as a quibbler.

Elsewhere he was rejected for other reasons.

Some colleges classified him as a pariah from Bombay; an Untouchable. More liberal schools refused to admit him unless he changed his color, gender, speech, and genealogy. He had to be black or red, female or androgynous, deaf and dumb. Consequently, in one school at least, Malunkyaputta was obliged to appear as a black young lady, a hermaphrodite who audited her gurus in total silence. In other schools, concerned with balancing their budget, he was rejected as a mendicant. His global credit card and universal passport, along with his poet's license, were stamped "invalid." As a result, he lived meagerly, on a bowl of gruel, Gandhi's survival diet, and was often homeless and hungry.

Despite these difficulties, Malunkyaputta pursued his studies for seven years. In addition to auditing the most advanced scholars, he pored over the leading newspapers, which he found in public libraries, subway stations, or the lobbies of hotels. He scanned the *London Times*, the *Washington Post*, the Wall Street Journal; he skimmed *L'Osservatore Romano*, the *Revue de Trois Mondes*, along with the *Sacramento Bee* and the *Miami Herald*. Though packed with misinformation, the newspapers revealed the world's current history hour by hour in more detail. The reporters resembled messengers of doom with choruses of senile graybeards or hysterical Cassandras in an endless Greek soap opera. They brought daily accounts of murder, rape, acts of terror, civil war; they told of riots, massacres, and famine, with children dying of hunger day after day.

Everywhere, the schools and jails and hospitals were overflowing. Great cities were turning into jungles.

Behind the ever-mounting tide of corruption, a brute fact was increasingly obvious: *the Earth was becoming dangerously overcrowded.* In spite of recurrent disasters-earthquakes, floods, fires; famines, plagues, and wars-more people inhabited the planet than ever before. And they kept multiplying. In this respect at least, they observed a biblical commandment: "Replenish the earth and multiply…"

Malunkyaputta pondered the prospects for the millennium. An Earth with ten billion inhabitants, fighting for food and space, struggling to survive. Anyone could foresee the future: the steady loss of human rights; the loss of privacy; the erosion of democracy; the steady increase in crimes of all kinds. Was there a solution to overcrowding? A cure for hunger and suffering? Could he, Malunkyaputta, find the right solution?

He made notes of his observations in his travel diary: as always, he composed poems and fables to edify himself...

* * *

While still an auditor at Oxford, Malunkyaputta heard about a special program free to all: A reading by three visiting poets, each of whom was a Nobel laureate.

Hoping to learn something edifying, he slipped into a church-like hall which seemed deserted. Except for Malunkyaputta, no one was anxious to hear the distinguished visitors. The three ancient parties sat on the platform, robed in black academic gowns, sunk in meditative silence. A man and two women. They seemed forlorn, almost otherworldly figures, yet somehow strangely familiar. Had Malunkyaputta known them in a former life? After introducing each other to the empty hall with appropriate eulogies, each read an excerpt from a prize work. Each read in a different style, in a whispering or portentous voice, with strains of the sublime mingling with the topical or the ridiculous. (The first laureate recited the final canto from his philosophical epic, *Naught I Sought*, in which he summarized his lifelong pursuit of Nirvana, or Nothingness. The second read from *Dido's Dildo*, her pornographic epic which projected a modern Dido's lament from her pyre and detailed her unquenchable lust. The third quoted passages from *The Undeliverable*, a biological epic which traced the poet's evolution as a fetus. "I'm here and now, to be sure," was the refrain. "Yet an embryo. Waiting to be born. And *Waiting to be Unborn*... Undeceived. To end a deceptive cycle...")

Before them, in the shadows of the Gothic hall, stood a ghostly company of earlier poets — Milton, Marvell, Donne, among others — who had visited the same hall, delivered fresh glory to English poetry, and seemed puzzled by their successors.

After the reading, Malunkyaputta went up to the platform to congratulate the laureates. They smiled at him distantly and thanked him politely. Then, assuming that he was another ambitious new poet, they warned him against pursuing poetry.

"It's a mug's game," said one, a stout old woman. "Fit for bearded old ladies, poor Jews, mad Irishmen, and other queer ducks...Too many would-be poets, not enough dead ones." Said her companion, "The best ones are dead. And no one reads them anymore...The field's overcrowded. It ought to be abolished..." The third laureate, who resembled Padman-Ananda, warned him emphatically: "Avoid poetry, young man, whatever you do. Avoid it like the latest Egyptian plague!"

Malunkyaputta looked at the laureates sadly.

"I appreciate your warning," he said. "But I cannot accept your advice. I aim to become a *universal* poet. I'd speak the truth for all mankind. 'I am a man,' said Terence, 'and nothing that is human is alien to me —'"

"Terence? But Terence is dead!" said the third laureate.

"That's a matter of opinion," said Malunkyaputta. "I have a message to deliver."

The laureates looked at him with raised eyebrows.

"A message?" cried one painfully. "But messages are out-of-date!"

"The best ones have been delivered!" cried another.

"No one listens to them," said the third, "no one wants to hear them!"

All chimed in, scoring the message-makers:

"Moses proclaimed his laws —"

"Jesus delivered his news —"

"Buddha showed the right way —"

"Zarathustra said 'Choose —'"

"Socrates said 'Examine —'"

"Galileo... Marx... Nietzsche —"

"All delivered messages —"

"'Choose! ... Refrain! ... Obey — !'"

"'Examine! ... Overcome! ... Follow me!'"

"The same old pious and preposterous exhortations — !"

"Who listens to messages?"

The laureates stared at deluded Malunkyaputta.

"All the same," said Malunkyaputta, "I aim to deliver my message. To free men from bondage. To cure them of their unhappiness."

"You seem to have messianic cravings," said the third laureate, glancing at the dark young man with measuring eyes. "Are you one of the Chosen perhaps? Bene Israel?"

"I don't know," said Malunkyaputta. "I've been called all sorts of names."

"The Chosen are always with us, awaiting their Messiah. And each of the Rejected thinks the Messiah might be himself. Pursuing delusions is a dangerous business, my friend."

"Too many poets," added his colleagues. "Burning with messages. The worst ones keep multiplying. More poets now than ever before."

*　*　*

Perplexed by the gurus in Oxford, Malunkyaputta visited the Bodleian Library where he looked up the records of noted Indian poets and sages. He scanned the manuscripts of Rabindranath Tagore, Sarvepalli Radhakrishnan, Ghosh Aurobindo, all of whom had studied or taught at Oxford. Searching for other models to emulate, he consulted Mahatma Gandhi's memoirs, *My Experiment with Truth*. The great soul had led the emancipation of India from Britain. He was, in a sense, the Messiah of India. And Malunkyaputta wondered: Should he go on a pilgrimage to New Delhi or Benares and commune with the gurus of India? But his destination depended on his karma, and this pointed in another direction.

As he walked down Oxford Street and passed by Blackwell's book shop, he noticed a new travel agency. Behind the plate glass window three busy travel agents seemed to be waving to him, beckoning him to enter. Malunkyaputta stepped inside.

"Your passport's ready, young man," said the first agent, a stout old lady in a flowery smock. "Your tickets are waiting..."

"My passport?" Malunkyaputta was puzzled.

"To the Holy Land," said the second agent, a short dark gentleman with appraising eyes. "To Mount Zion in Jerusalem."

"Jerusalem?" Malunkyaputta echoed him.

"It's the place to go this year," said the second agent. "For your edification... Next year it may not be available."

"A good school for poets and prophets," said the third agent, a young beauty who smiled at Malunkyaputta with star-bright eyes. "A school for curing the blind and raising the dead..."

So Malunkyaputta was guided toward the Holy Land.

Chapter II. The Pilgrim

Using his passport, he journeyed toward Jerusalem from London by ship and rail via Brussels, Vienna, Belgrade, Haifa, and Tel-Aviv. Tel-Aviv was a new Jewish town next to the old seaport Jaffa where the reluctant prophet Jonah had tried to escape his mission to Nineveh; he was swallowed by a whale, then regurgitated. Malunkyaputta took a local train from Tel-Aviv to Jerusalem which lay some thirty miles southeast of the Mediterranean coast. It was spring in Israel near the time of the Passover, the seventh year after the founding of the old-new state.

David's old fortress-city was built on Mount Zion, a craggy hilltop among other hills which rose about 2000 feet above sea level and had survived earthquakes, sieges, and other cataclysms. The place was surrounded by huge boulders, tortured rocks, and steep valleys of stones. It bore the rubble and ruin of walls from the times of Solomon, Herod, Pontius Pilate, Titus, the Roman legions, the Crusaders, Richard the Lion-hearted, and Saladin the Magnificent. (Columbus had sought gold in the Indies, partly to finance a new crusade for the recovery of Jerusalem.) Around the old city a vast desert stretched southward to Mount Sinai and the Saharas. The desert was part of an evaporating sea's bottom, a residue of which was the Dead Sea, fed by a trickle from the River Jordan, a few miles east of Jerusalem.

Malunkyaputta climbed Mount Zion and surveyed the remains from the past. Within these stony acres Jeremiah had mourned the invasion of Nebuchadnezzar. Within the same area Jesus had celebrated a last passover in Herod's Temple. Malunkyaputta made his pilgrimage through the much-divided city.

Like thousands of pilgrims since the time of Helena, the mother of Constantine, he visited the sacred sites. He made his way through a maze of alleys packed with tourists, the stalls of fruit-sellers, the venders of souvenirs — selling slivers from the Cross, a thorn from the Crown, a hair from the beard of Nicodemus. The place resembled an Oriental bazaar. Street signs reported the Stations of the Cross, the Via Dolorosa of Jesus on his way to his crucifixion as king of the Jews.

He passed the Church of the Holy Sepulchre, built on the site of Golgotha. He passed the Dome of the Rock, the golden mosque of Omar which marked the place from which the prophet Mohammed had ascended into Paradise on a white horse, according to Moslem tradition. He passed by David's Citadel and the King David Hotel, an ultra-modern hotel a stone's throw from the Dome of the Rock.

Malunkyaputta meditated on Jesus: a mystical poet, his own family considered him mad. A descendant of David, Jesus had been reared in the teachings of Moses who reportedly carved the Decalog on Mt. Sinai. The two most important commandments, Jesus believed, were first to love and worship only one God and, second, to love your neighbor as yourself, as stated in Leviticus. The second was perhaps the hardest commandment. He believed that the end of the world was imminent. He lived in a time of deepening troubles when Rome and its tax-collectors wielded harsh power over a poor occupied province. A visionary poet, he perceived his neighbors' spiritual desolation. He spoke to them in his passionate, often paradoxical, sayings and parables, which were his poems. His listeners, who were few in the beginning, remembered his words. Later, his message, his miraculous cures, his tragic end, and his reported resurrection shaped the accounts of his life in Mark, Matthew, Luke and John. In time, many Jews, and many among the poor Greek and Roman slaves who had heard Paul's sermons accepted Jesus as their messiah. In time, much of the decaying empire was converted to Christianity, the faith of those who called themselves Christianos or the followers of Jesus the Christ, originally an orthodox Jew and a miracle-worker.

* * *

Malunkyaputta knew the ancient history of the Hebrews. The Five Books of Moses, from Genesis to Deuteronomy, furnished clues as to how and why they became a peculiar people. When the Jews were enslaved in Egypt, they were forced to bake bricks without straw, to help build the pyramids for a new Pharaoh, and the Jews complained. Moses tried to persuade the Pharaoh to let the Jews escape from bondage. But the Pharaoh, who may have been Rameses II the empire builder, held to his higher vision. "The pyramids are my best public works project," he declared. "They are my eternal monuments, my everlasting survival shelters. The Jews must help to build them or else, by Toth, I'll drown them in the Nile!"

Moses then engaged in a contest with the Pharaoh's priests and magicians. He afflicted Egypt with the Ten Plagues, which threatened the whole kingdom. "The Jews are my worst plague!" the Pharaoh cried at last. "Get them out of Egypt!" Moses did. He lead the Exodus, "in a cloud by day and a pillar of fire by night," an event which may have been linked to the cataclysmic earthquakes and volcanic eruptions which had sunk Atlantis and shattered Crete.

After crossing the Red Sea the Jews started to complain again: they missed the fleshpots of Egypt. Moses promised them manna, and the manna came. But the Jews got tired of manna. Moses, tired of his Chosen, gave them his Decalog, the Ten Commandments. The Jews broke the stone tablets which Moses had carved on Mount Sinai. They raised the Golden Calf in tribute to the Bull God of Egypt and, hoping to increase the fertility of their flocks, danced the hora around it. In punishment, Moses gave them 600 additional commandments and fenced them into the Promised Land. Ever since, the Jews have been peculiar.

*   *   *

Malunkyaputta stood by the Wailing Wall, left over from Herod's Temple, and watched the ingathering of the chosen. The survivors of holocausts came from ghettos in Poland and Russia. They came from the capitals of Europe. They came from distant parts of the earth. Some came from Minsk or Odessa; some from Baghdad, Budapest, Brooklyn; some from Lisbon, London, Rio de Janeiro. Some came from Yemen and Ethiopia; some from Palm Springs; some from Sodom and Gomorrha. They came from diverse lands with diverse speech and customs, all moving Zionward as if borne on eagles' wings. They gathered by the mute stone blocks of the wall and, swaying back and forth, raised their voices in a kaddish to their inscrutable god.

"Lord of the Universe," they prayed. "Are you home on Mount Zion again? Can you hear us? Israel has returned! Your chosen people, a remnant of remnants, long suffering in exile, long suffered by the Gentiles and our insufferable neighbors: Israel, your Suffering Servant People, is back by the wall. We are trying to read the message in the rock; trying to decode the small print in our old contract with you; trying to interpret the numerous clauses in our covenant. The text is so worn it's almost invisible.

"Can you hear us, O Master of the Universe? Why have you chosen us for your peculiar treasure? What have we done to deserve your notice? What new disaster are you planning to test us with? Who will deliver us from terror and fear; the sharp stones of our neighbors; the rage and hate of our multiplying enemies? When and where shall we find peace?"

*   *   *

The Zionists who had survived Hitler's holocaust were now threatened with annihilation by the Arabs. After some 2000 years in exile, the world's oldest refugees had reclaimed their biblical homeland (which Yahweh had promised Abraham) and established the modern State of Israel in 1948. The returning Jews built roads, schools, hospitals, factories. The Kibbutzim drained the swamps; planted forests, orchards, vineyards, olive and orange groves; they irrigated the desert. In doing so, they displaced the Arabs who had lived in Palestine for centuries. The Arabs swore to destroy the invaders and drive Israel into the sea. The Jews fought bitter battles against the surrounding Arab countries, Egypt, Syria, Jordan, Lebanon, and resisted their enemies. Though vastly outnumbered, they maintained their hold and continued to occupy the Promised Land.

The old feud between the Jews and the Arabs is reported in the first chapters of Genesis. According to the Bible, which many claim to be the word of God, Abraham of Ur was the father of both Isaac and Ishmael. Isaac became the ancestor of the Jews; Ishmael, the ancestor of the Arabs: The two Semitic people were blood brothers, although Ishmael's mother Hagar was said to have been an Egyptian concubine of Abraham. After Noah and the Great Flood, Jehovah commanded them to be fruitful and multiply. "Populate the earth abundantly... I will multiply your seed as the stars of heaven and as the sand on the seashore..."

Observing this commandment, the descendants of both Isaac and Ishmael multiplied. The early Jews, who roamed in the wastelands for generations in search of greener pastures for their flocks, resembled the roving Bedouins of Palestine who pursue their ancestral way of life to this day. Sitting around their camp fires or in their black goat-skin tents, they told each other fables in the style of the Arabian Nights Tales to explain all the mysteries under a star-studded heaven. The Jews imagined a god who gave them Moses for their prophet, rescued them from slavery in Egypt and chose them for his peculiar treasure. The Arabs became animated by their prophet Mohammed around 600 A.D. In the name of Allah and Mohammed, his one true prophet, they conquered and converted to Islam millions of people in Africa, Europe, Asia, even as far as India, where the Muslims taught the Koran, built great mosques and schools and centers of learning. Later, when oil was found in Arabia, many formerly poor Arab countries became immensely rich. They were able to buy modern weapons, from bombers to rocket-launchers, in their war against the Jews. Indeed, thought Malunkyaputta, same remarkable things had been done, in the name of rival prophets and poets.

*   *   *

Pursuing his quest for edification, Malunkyaputta visited the Hebrew University. It had treasures of all sorts, donated by rich merchants from nearly every nation. Monumental bronze doors at the entrance; a hall with stained glass windows by Chagall, remembering the wonder-working rabbis of the shtetl. In the library the People of the Book were industriously translating all the best old and new books of the world into Hebrew. The Zionists had resurrected Hebrew as their national language, a long-dead language written from right to left in ancient cuneiform. (They despised Yiddish as a medieval German jargon and a hangover from the ghetto.) They were transferring their Hebrew translations into microfilm, which they stored in bomb-proof shelters below the library.

Malunkyaputta looked at a special exhibit of the Dead Sea Scrolls which displayed the oldest known scrolls of the prophet Isaiah. The rare parchments had been discovered in 1947 by a Bedouin boy who was searching for his lost sheep in the caves above the Dead Sea near Jericho. They had been hidden in clay jars by the Essenes, a sect of otherworldly Jews who may have included John the Baptist... The library had other treasures in its archives: letters from the Pharaoh Akhenaten's agent at Tel el-Amarna; a letter allegedly from the Queen of Sheba to Solomon... It had a more recent letter from Bene Israel in Bombay which asked permission for Hindu Jews to return to the Promised Land. Another letter from a synagogue of Chinese Jews in Kaifeng which also invoked the Law of Return; this allowed any Jew to claim residence in Israel. The Chinese Jews observed the rules of Moses, they wrote; they circumcised their sons; they refused to eat pork. They hoped to escape from the restrictions of life in crowded China.

Malunkyaputta visited the Knesset, or Parliament, which had 120 members and nearly as many parties. Sitting below a blow-up photo of Teodor Herzl (a frustrated Viennese playwright who, suffering from delusions of grandeur, had cast himself as a second Moses), Malunkyaputta listened to the arguments between the messianic rabbis and the militant atheists. They were trying to solve the problem of making peace with the Arabs while expanding the Jewish colonies to the banks of the Euphrates and preparing for war, for Armageddon, and/or the advent of the Messiah...

Malunkyaputta visited Yad-Vashem, a plaza dedicated to Holocaust Memorials. Many Jews had brought stones to the plaza: small stones, wrapped in newspapers from all parts of the world. With these stones they intended to build a tower, taller than the pyramids, as a perpetual reminder of the Holocaust. Others were designing a scroll for a cloud-scraping wall, a scroll with Six Million Names engraved in stone, as a memorial to the martyrs.

* * *

Inspecting Yad-Vashem, three rabbis were arguing about a proper memorial service for the victims of Auschwitz. Rabbi Moishe declared that, after the Holocaust, the old contract from Mount Sinai was no longer valid. The Jews were no longer the Chosen People. Any memorial service was bound to be a fraud.

Rabbi Buber admitted that Jehovah was dead. He had choked to death on the fumes of his Chosen from the chimneys in Auschwitz. The long I-Thou dialog was finished. Any service should be held in total silence.

Rabbi Adolf claimed that he had done the most to carry out Jehovah's program for the Jews. The result of the Holocaust was the Return to Zion. Hence he, Rabbi Adolf, not Rabbi Herzl, was the true Founding Father of Israel. Any memorial must give Rabbi Adolf chief credit for the restoration or the Resurrection of Israel.

Unable to agree on this, the rabbis parted company.

* * *

Before leaving Yad-Vashem, Rabbi Buber told a little story, known to both the Pharaoh Rameses II and Chancellor Hitler as *The Oldest Problem* or *The Final Solution*:

"One dictator expelled all the priests from his country. Another exiled all poets and philosophers. A third removed bankers, lawyers and pawnbrokers. A fourth liquidated the Jews.

"The last dictator explained: 'By liquidating the Jews I cured all the plagues that can afflict a country. I removed the chief sources of disturbances. I removed the circulators of fake hopes and false promises. I removed the chronic distributors of counterfeit goods and evils, messianic dreams and delusions. In other words, I removed our most troublesome critics. By liquidating the Jews, I solved our chief problems. Our country may seem like a prison to the world, but it is clean, quiet, and fairly comfortable.' "

*   *   *

Malunkyaputta had his own views of the Holocaust. As a would-be prophet, he tried to emulate Isaiah and score the grievance-collectors. (Isaiah had sought to comfort and reform God's Suffering Servant People Israel and was the prophet whom Jesus had studied most closely.) In a mixed crowd of tourists, Passover pilgrims, and kaddish-chanting believers, Malunkyaputta tested his prophetic voice as a mouthpiece for Jehovah, and spoke above the hubbub in front of Yad-Vashem:

"What to me is the multitude to your sacrifices?" says the Lord. "I have had enough of burnt offerings… Build me no Holocaust Museums! Engrave me no lists of Six Million Names. I need no reminders of your sufferings. Nor of your iniquities… Your memorials are not acceptable to me. I hate the smell of your sacrifices... A people utterly estranged, I will not listen to you…"

A bearded old Jew with sharp ears — he may have been Rabbi Kahn, a disciple of Mendel Schneerson of Brooklyn or the Chief Rabbi of Jerusalem — overheard his remarks and was scandalized. He wore a long black coat, a fur hat in medieval Polish style, and carried a cane.

He peered into Malunkyaputta's swarthy face and quizzed him with his Four-and-Twenty Questions:

Are you one of the Chosen?
Is your mother kosher?
Have you been redeemed?
Have you been circumcised?

Malunkyaputta saw the gleam in the old man's eyes (they now reminded of Padman) and gave him fuzzy answers, which he considered diplomatic:

"I cannot tell you, I'm sorry… Just *who* is a Jew?

"I never met my mother…

"I can't believe all I hear and see. Can you?"

"I've never been sold. So how could I be redeemed?"

The zealous old Jew, frowning with righteous indignation, lived in a mythological world and believed in the Torah as firmly as a physicist might believe in Einstein's formulas. He shook his cane at Malunkyaputta. "Oy veh!" he cried. "Mocker of the Law and the Prophets! Compounder of confusion! How dare you profane our Holy Land? Am ha-aretz!" He sputtered an appropriate curse and raised his cane to strike down the blasphemer.

Malunkyaputta knocked the cane from the rabbi's hand and left Jerusalem.

He had hoped to learn the art of the old poet-prophets. He wanted to say a few wonderful new things to solace an old unhappy people, things which they could believe and wish to remember. But he saw that the Holy Land was a realm of fables. The Zionists were a band of mad poets. They were dancing on coals of fire in a kingdom of the absurd.

*   *   *

A skeptical pilgrim, he wandered in the desert far south of Jerusalem. Confused by mirages, he lost himself in the wilderness of Shur, beyond Beersheba, a desolate region without any water.

Increasingly thirsty, he stumbled for days through a shimmering wasteland of sand. The hot wind parched and blackened his skin. At times he was delirious. At times he chanted to himself in a croaking voice:

> The old springs are polluted, the waters bitter;
> > the wells choked with sand...
> What happens to him who goes forth to find a new spring?
> > What happens to him who goes too far alone
> > > in a tumult of winds in a land of sand and ashes?
> > Will he lose himself in a springless world?

Near noon one day he saw a dark shadow flying overhead like a huge metallic vulture. It was a jet plane speeding toward the south. Was it the Concorde on a round-the-world flight? For a moment Malunkyaputta thought he saw a solitary passenger waving to him from behind a row of small round port-holes. And he thought he recognized the passenger. It seemed to be his Precious Lady Step-Mother, stout and gross like the Ugly Duchess. She was surveying him through her glittering binoculars. She was waving to him, pointing to the south as if urging him to go in that direction; then she pointed north as if she had changed her mind. A moment later the plane vanished on the far horizon.

Malunkyaputta stumbled southward until he reached an oasis called Marah. But it was a barren oasis, for its spring waters were salt-encrusted and bitter. The rocks around the black pool were surrounded by unearthly pillars of salt, carved by the desert winds over centuries. A lean man in white was kneeling by the pool, testing the bitter water. A chemist on a mission from Hebrew University, he resembled Padman-Ananda, his old critic from the ashram.

"What are we doing here?" Malunkyaputta asked in a daze.

"Testing. Testing and tasting the water... Pursuing the obvious. As ever..."

"What have we discovered?"

"The obvious, of course! A cure for hunger perhaps..."

"What good will it do?"

"It may reduce suffering. For a little while..."

The strange yet familiar scientist then explained his discovery. "The waters of Marah are the same as the waters of the Dead Sea. Though 200 miles apart, the springs of both are a part of the same underground ocean. An aquifer, trapped after the last Ice Age. The bitter waters can be reclaimed and used to raise crops. They can be used to feed millions of people in the deserts of the world..."

Malunkyaputta turned from the mirage and wandered in another direction in circling northward through the endless, solitary desert.

* * *

Days later, blinded by sand storms and devoured by thirst, he found himself lying on the shores of the Dead Sea. His robe was in rags; his body resembled a carcass. He was stinking like Lazarus of Bethany on the third day in the tomb. The sea before him was ringed with eroding hills and cliffs. The cliffs held the caves where the Essenes had hidden their apocalyptic scrolls.

Gazing up the road to Jericho with delirious eyes, Malunkyaputta thought he saw a beautiful young woman approaching, floating in green silk veils, shimmering with finery like the Queen of Sheba. Mia seemed to him more beautiful than ever, and he thought he heard her calling to him, singing the Song of Songs:

"Arise, my love, and come away... I seek him whom my soul loves... Set me as a seal upon your heart for love is strong as death... Many waters cannot quench love, neither can floods drown it..."

He answered her with whispered lines he had composed in a former life:

> I cannot claim to make your beauty deathless:
> Your singing self will long outlast my rhyme.
> From words I build no cage to catch your breathless
> Music, unbetrayable by time.
>
> I cannot boast my love will prove immortal:
> The pyramids are crumbling with the moon,
> And time will find the greenest garden portal
> To choke with sand the flowers of night or noon.
>
> We walked the hills in another world one evening
> And ate red apples by a pool of stars:
> Like playful gods who send the planets wheeling,
> We flung our apple-cores at Mors or Mars.
> And since I could not trap eternities
> I caught but that one moment: here it is.

Mia sat by him for a long moment and held his cadaverous hand as if to console him in his last pangs.

"Alas," she said with a sigh, "our moments are a part of Eternity... They recur and pass and return again. The same, yet ever-changing, for the children of Time... For me, the old enchantments will not do..."

Mia smiled at him remotely, as if she heard another more distant yet more impelling song, then rose and left him, fading away on the road to Jericho. A shimmering image of beauty, a mirage by the Dead Sea, she resembled the Queen of Sheba and, at the same time, a dusky whore from Jericho.

On the verge of expiring, Malunkyaputta tried to fortify himself. "I aim to die well," he repeated to himself like a mantra. I traveled far, in search of edification, tasting both good and evil. I caught a glimpse of the beautiful... My time's running out and I haven't delivered my message... Yet a death died well is well died for all time... I aim to die well..." He tried to compose his last words, as a poet dying of thirst by the sea, or as a skeptical pilgrim bidding farewell to a much-promised land, but his mind was becoming confused.

"Adieu, old Song of Songs," he muttered. "Farewell, old book of psalms and lamentations... Farewell, Father Abram, who begot both Isaac and Ishmael, his ever-quarreling sons... Farewell, Job on his dung hill; Moses the Egyptian, and Zipporah who circumcised him... Lot's wife who turned into a pillar of salt... Farewell Isaiah, sawn over a barrel; Jeremiah, dumped into a cesspool; Ezekiel levitating over a valley of dead bones. Hosea who married a whore. Malachi who promised a messiah... Farewell Marah, the Jordan, the stones of Jerusalem. Farewell the Dead Sea. Farewell, O Kingdom of the Absurd! The wind that blew from Sinai blows dust and sand...."

So he rambled for awhile, then told himself firmly: "I aim to die well."

But before he could accomplish this last worthy though desperate enterprise, he had a brief but remarkable vision which changed his situation.

Chapter III. The Inventor

On the verge of dying of thirst by the Dead Sea, Malunkyaputta dreamt of a faucet, a faucet with a filter which converted saltwater into sweetwater. It was a prophetic vision or, more accurately, a scientific prognostication. In this, Malunkyaputta resembled Professor Mendeleyev of Petersburg who dreamed up several missing elements in the periodic table; Professor Kekule of Stadonitz who discovered the structure of benzene rings in a dream and won a Nobel prize; Professor Sagan who dreamed he heard voices calling him from Mars and Venus and established a listening station to report the voices.

Within the brief interval or narrow passage of his dream Malunkyaputta fitted his faucet with a valve which arrested the molecules of salt and vaporized the sodium into a harmless gas, less harmful than carbon monoxide or Zyklon-B. Fixed to a short metal pipe, the miraculous spigot could be driven into the beach or coast of any sea, however salty, and would produce an unlimited supply of sweet water. His invention obviously filled a universal need. A triumph of applied science, the faucet not only quenched men's thirst and relieved them from suffering dehydration. It could turn the earth's deserts into flourishing new Gardens of Eden and yield an endless supply of fresh fruits and vegetables and crops of all kinds. It would abolish thirst and hunger forever.

Though his dream was short, Malunkyaputta caught a glimpse of its promise and fortune favored him. On the brink of dying he was rescued by a pair of wandering Samaritans. They lifted him onto a hump of their camel and took him to a hostel in Jericho. They nursed him back to life. When Malunkyaputta told them about his faucet, they marveled at his wonderful invention. Then they called one of their cousins, an Egyptian lawyer in Washington who, in exchange for a small percentage from future profits, helped Malunkyaputta to secure a patent for it. With the patent Malunkyaputta was able to interest a manufacturer, who had branches in Cairo, Baghdad, Teheran, Tokyo, Taiwan, Mexico City, and the manufacturer set up factories to make millions of faucets with the miraculous filter for worldwide distribution. Within a short time Malunkyaputta was collecting endless royalties. Within a short time he was a billionaire.

*   *   *

Pursuing his quest for edification, Malunkyaputta now resolved to taste and test all the traditional pleasures of a bona fide billionaire. He toured the world, visiting exotic places, from Galapagos to Easter Island, from Bali to Capri, from Papua to Patagonia. He stayed in the grandest hotels. He took part in the usual sports: golf, tennis, horseback riding, jogging, skiing, wind-surfing, mud baths and sauna. He ate in the best gourmet restaurants, grills, baboon bars. He moved in a cloud of masseurs, barbers, beauticians, dietitians. He learned that the rich spent much of their time eating and resting; eating and reducing; eating and complaining. The poor did much the same, of course, but on a more modest scale. He visited the casinos, gift shops, museums. He visited the Rejuvenation Centers where the guests could enjoy the replacement of vital parts. Injections of new drugs for sex-recharge, endurance and longevity. They could also enjoy sex-change, from male to female and vice versa, for a fresh variety of pleasures.

As a result of his sporting life, Malunkyaputta became increasingly handsome and charismatic. Everywhere he went he was treated with the respect and deference which only a genuine billionaire deserves. His opinions on any subject were received as revelations; and even his casual remarks were quoted as the brightest sayings since the time of King Midas.

Before long, however, Malunkyaputta became bored with the grand hotels. The routine seemed to him an endless round of games and charades at an infinite Baboon's Bar. He grew weary of the bland hypocritical faces of his valets and fellow tycoons. "I am rich," he told himself. "I can buy anything I want. There must be something better..." He investigated other sources of pleasure. Acquiring private properties, he bought townhouses in London, Paris, Rome, Beverly Hills. He bought a mile-long yacht, jet planes, a Bentley, a hundred new suits and shoes, a dozen Rolex watches. He bought a casino in Las Vegas for games; an opera house in San Francisco for private recitals. He bought a model agency and slept with a different beauty queen every night. He gratified his most extravagant desires and fantasies.

31

No need to list all his pleasures. With an unlimited bank account, almost anyone can draw up a list to stagger even Sardanapalus who raised the Hanging Gardens of Babylon, once among the seven wonders of the world. The more money Malunkyaputta spent, the more his fortune grew, for water was more plentiful than oil, and his miraculous faucet yielded seemingly inexhaustible revenues. His chief problem was how to use his ever-increasing wealth in a way that was durably satisfying.

During his prosperous interlude as a billionaire, he kept a private office in Hollywood, not far from Howard Hughes' hideaway, where his staff included his chief accountant, Mr. Padman; his financial advisor and fortune-teller, Madam Marah; and his confidential secretary, the beauteous and elusive Miss Mia...

* * *

On his thirtieth birthday Malunkyaputta gave a grand party aboard his yacht, anchored near Crete. In addition to a pair of stout but senescent fellow billionaires from Newport Beach, he invited some of his former associates, a sheik from Saudi Arabia, the laureates from Oxford, the chief rabbi of Jerusalem, the Good Samaritans from Jericho, diplomats from the United Nations with their beautiful ladies. Those who responded to his invitation were provided with hydroplanes to Crete for quick transportation.

The colorful guests assembled, bearing an assortment of rare gifts. Very handsome in his white naval uniform, with the air of a great rajah or a Hindu Prince, Malunkyaputta welcomed his distinguished visitors with democratic impartiality. A feast of delicacies was served in the yacht's great dining hall and ballroom. A string trio played Radhakrishnan's virtuoso variations on *Happy Birthday to You*. Then three singers, wearing clowns' masks, emerged from an enormous birthday cake to sing their fulsome congratulations. They were joined by the guests who stood and raised their glasses to Malunkyaputta, singing in a resonant chorus:

> Happy Birthday, Malunkyaputta,
> Happy Birthday to You!
> Our hero's performed a marvelous feat:
> He found a need and filled the need.
> His faucet made the desert green!

He fed the hungry, filled the poor,
Multiplied bread and raised the dead.
All glory to our Wonder-Worker;
Malunkyaputta the Magnificent!
Happy Birthday to You!

Malunkyaputta was overwhelmed. He wanted to express his thanks for the rare gifts and the great tribute, but found himself speechless. Tears trickled from his lustrous eyes. Glowing with pride and happiness, he bowed to his guests in silent gratitude. He had indeed reached the peak of mortal happiness. What more could he desire?

The three clowns now drew him aside and removed their masks. They presented him with their small private gifts: a rice bowl, a lotus bud, a hair from the head of the Buddha. They gazed at him reproachfully. They resembled his old friends from a former life. They sang to him softly, in whispering voices:

What happened to you, Malunkyaputta?
So rich, yet so terribly poor...
Have you deceived yourself again,
repeating the games of the past?
Have you forgotten your mission?
To become a poet and raise the veil;
to teach the sad truth of things;
to heal the suffering poor?

Malunkyaputta looked at the three strangers in confusion. They seemed to be singing a strange yet familiar song:

Tantra, mantra, dharma, karma—
Pad-mini, chit-rini, Pad-man, Anan-da...
Mia-mayah, mu-dita, ku-data...
Ma-rah, ma-rah; Dhira-dhira—
Tantra, mantra, dharma, karma....

He could hardly believe his ears.

Then one of the singers approached him confidentially. A homely old woman in fashionable clothes, she had the critical air of a sharp-eyed dowager duchess, resembling Our Precious Lady Stepmother.

"Wake up, young man, it's time," she told him.

"I beg your pardon," said Malunkyaputta.

"Rid yourself of your vanities," she told him.

"I don't understand—"

"You never could see the obvious. Your miraculous faucet is a great blunder. It breeds new multitudes who must die of hunger. You've added to the sum of human suffering."

"I can't believe my ears," said Malunkyaputta.

"Believe neither your ears nor your eyes," said the old woman. "Wake from your dreams and delusions. It's time. Time to give up your riches, time to take up your mission—"

"My mission?"

"To teach the truth and deliver your message. Let your birthday be the death-day of your delusions. Let it be the day of your awakening!"

She turned from him with a reproachful glance and seemed to fade into the sea fog, along with her two companions, and along with all the transient guests at the party.

Malunkyaputta found himself alone. Was he dreaming again, or was he awakening?

* * *

He was drifting on a deserted yacht in a sea of fog; for a night and a day he was drifting at sea in danger of drowning. He was painfully aware of the truth of his visitors' accusations. He had indeed wasted his time. Pursuing his pleasures he had increased the sum of human suffering. The faucet which had turned the wastelands into bountiful gardens had increased the number of the poor. It had multiplied by the millions the mouths that were insatiably hungry. All the efforts to increase the yields were not enough to keep up with the needs of the ever-multiplying poor.

At the same time, he felt confused and puzzled by many things. If he gave up his fortune, would that help the poor? A hundred billion dollars, divided among ten billion of the poor, would furnish each with ten dollars. This would not last long. The poor were simply breeding too fast. The solution would bankrupt any billionaire, yet fail to satisfy the poor. "The poor are always with us," Malunkyaputta told himself.

"Yet so are the rich." The rich are needier and greedier perhaps. Having more soap, they smell sweeter. But the poor have talent too. In time, they could learn to fart as fragrantly as the rich. In time, they could vote the rich into extinction. Yet that wouldn't solve the problem. The poor breed faster...

> The more the cake, the more the flies.
> The more the bread, the more they breed.
> The more they breed, the more must die.

Malunkyaputta knew that he must give up his riches. He must launch his mission. The poor must be enlightened. They must be emancipated. They must be saved from recurrent suffering.

Yet a part of him was not quite ready to take the last step. Was it truly the *right* way to give up his enormous wealth, to strip himself naked and put on a mendicant preacher's rags? A part of him was allergic to the hungry and homeless, the spreading legions of the poor. An ever-growing army of breeders threatened to over-run the earth and devour every inch of living space.

Had he explored all the ways in coping with the problem? Something important was eluding his understanding.

Chapter IV. The Philanthropist

Before giving up his riches, Malunkyaputta decided to use his wealth in an all-out effort to find a solution to the population problem. Always anxious to emulate the best models, he studied the examples of the most benevolent billionaires, from Carnegie, Ford and Rockefeller to Getty, Gulbenkian, and Guggenheim; he meditated on the lives of noble philanthropists, from Aga Khan to the Maharaja of Benares. Some of them had set up foundations for the general improvement of mankind. Some of them granted enormous sums for promoting religion, education, health, art, science, astrology and cultural diversity. Tax exempt, the foundations did much to preserve the founder's name, perpetuate his views and, incidentally, provide jobs for his less distinguished relatives. The founders were to be remembered, like Hammurabi the People's Friend who carved his legend on a stele in Babylonia along with the code of justice he received from the hands of Shamash, a forgotten god. The foundations themselves, however, did not do much to improve mankind, which continued to multiply and degenerate, the worst breeding much faster than the best.

After further meditation, Malunkyaputta decided to use his fortune to set up his own foundation and conduct a global contest. He offered alluring prizes for the best solutions to the problem of over breeding. The ten prizes, each amounting to a billion dollars in cash, were bigger than the Ford and Rockefeller or the Gates-Getty-Gulbenkian awards. The competition was open to all, without any strings. The judges were incorruptible; they were monitored by the Supreme Court, the World Court, the Council of the United Nations, and the Federal Reserve Bank's Board of Governors.

Needless to say, the Malunkyaputta Foundation at its headquarters in The Hague was flooded with applications. More than a million proposals were submitted from every crowded town and village on earth. A staff of 200 rapid multi-lingual readers reviewed or scanned each application.

Most of the proposals fell into five familiar categories:

1. *Birth Control Devices.* These included the condom, the diaphragm, a fool-proof French pill, the Gregory Pincus Miracle Pill, and the Pope's infallible rhythm method. (One contestant proposed that Malunkyaputta's famous faucet be supplied with a chemical which, when combined with fresh water, would permanently sterilize anyone who drank it, without any side effects.)

2. *Abortion.* This cure was occasionally combined with detailed suggestions on the economic use of fetuses for food, medicine, parts replacement, or fertilizer. (The number of abortions performed each month was estimated at over 50,000 in New York alone.)

3. *Eugenics Programs.* These proposed gene engineering, cloning, and general stock control, in line with earlier Nazi experiments to improve the human race.

4. *Euthanasia.* The prompt and painless elimination of defectives and sociopaths, including dwarfs, gays, mutants, morons, and mental cases; welfare clients, parasites, malingerers; along with habitual liars, crooks, embezzlers, noise makers, deluders, polluters, robbers, rapists, and other criminals.

5. *Genocide.* The scientific liquidation of the more prolific inferior races and classes, including the reds, blacks, browns, yellows, pinks and substandard whites. Some added more specifically the Romanies, Armenians, Mongoloids; Hottentots, Bushmen, and Cannibals; Indians, Arabians, Siamese; Proletarians, Profiteers, Mammonites; Jews, Turks, Muslims; Baptists, Dunkards, Dippers and Shakers of every description. Some recommended the A-Bomb as the most promising contraceptive of the future.

Nearly all the proposed cures had been tried already, of course, and did not satisfy everyone. A prominent gambler in Nevada wired from Las Vegas: "The Pope's method is riskier than Russian roulette. Our casino is safer…" A philosopher in Pakistan, a eunuch by choice, wired from Multan: "Universal castration is the *only* practical solution!"

Critics in more distant places condemned Malunkyaputta and the contest itself.

A bishop wired from a conference in Cairo: "God himself proclaimed his law in Genesis: 'Replenish the Earth and multiply.' Your contest defies the laws of God and the Pope... Copulation is every man's sacred right!"

The president of the Emancipated Women's League, Dame Potiphar wired from Washington: "Your contest is unpatriotic. We must do all we can to expand our numbers. Let every man do his duty!"

A tribal chief wired from Dakar: "Your contest is part of a capitalistic conspiracy. A plot of white supremacists to reduce us. Let no one rob us of our least expensive pleasure and our last best right! We'll never give up our right to fuck; to fuck by day and fuck by night; to fuck and fuck as long as we like!"

*   *   *

Always eager to edify himself, Malunkyaputta reviewed other reports from the ever-expanding Third World, from Africa, South America, Asia. As a native of India, the world's poorest and most populous country, he considered himself an adept in the problems of over-population. Summarizing the brute facts of futurity, he drafted a decalog.

Millennial Warnings

1. At the present birth rate, the Earth's human population will exceed ten billion within a generation.

2. One-third of the surplus children will suffer hunger or die of starvation.

3. The population pressure will reduce the Earth's natural resources: crop lands, forests, pure water, pure air.

4. It will increase the pollution of the environment and cause the extinction of other species.

5. It will promote the growth of giant city slums, and the spreading of poverty like a global plague.

6. It will reduce human rights and the respect for life; democracy; dignity; privacy.

7. It will fuel hostility, hatred, violence; terrorism, civil war, and war at large.

8. Overbreeding will promote global warming and the greenhouse effect; it will cause floods and droughts; it will change the earth's climate.

9. It will lead to a degraded planet, less and less habitable, more and more savage.

10. It will condemn newborn millions to squalor, starvation, ignorance, and disease. It will add to the sum total of human suffering.

*　*　*

Padman-Ananda observed ruefully: "The contest is another delusion. If Krishna cannot prevail, Arjuna must fail...The uninhibitable will render the earth uninhabitable..."

Our Precious Lady Stepmother remarked: "The riddle has no solution. As long as man is born of woman, man pursues woman, and each must bear his own karma..."

Mia said with a sigh: "Did Buddha know the right way?"

*　*　*

Though the contest had failed to produce a practical and universal solution, Malunkyaputta awarded the grand prizes, as promised, to the lucky few. He presided at the dignified ceremony in The Hague, where he received the grateful thanks of the ten new billionaires politely, with a speculative smile.

Then, preparing to launch his mission, he closed the foundation and disposed of his fortune, including his patents for the faucet and future royalties. He sold his treasures and impedimenta: his townhouses and hideaways in London, Paris, Rome, Palm Springs, the Riviera; his yacht, his fleet of Bentleys and jet planes; his galleries, museums, casinos. He sold his cattle ranches in Patagonia, his rice plantations in Sumatra, his factories in Mexico and Singapore; and all the rest of his possessions. In effect, signs "For Sale," now covered his many mansions. (Some of the places were bought by retired clergymen and bankers who converted the mansions into orphanages for surplus children.)

A few of his treasures were bought by the Vatican. Some were sold in auction houses by Sothebys of London. Some went to the Guggenheims of Manhattan; some to the Gettys of Malibu. Some he transferred for future disposal to his old friends in Jericho who had invested in the faucet and founded the Global Bank of Good Samaritans, with active though anonymous clients in oil, copper, teak, plutonium, software, hardware, armaments, and Old Masters.

Malunkyaputta donated all his receipts and revenues, in hand or forthcoming, to the Smithsonian Institute as a trust fund for the promotion and improvement of Science. Having rid himself of his riches and converted himself into the poorest of the poor, he was ready to pursue his mission.

Preparing to enlighten the people, he reviewed his experience in his more recent incarnations: as pilgrim, inventor, philanthropist. Did he understand all or any of his lessons? Was he becoming properly edified? Was he pursuing the right way? Something important still seemed to be eluding him. He was perplexed by his mixed feelings. The recurrent horrors of history. The fascination of the absurd. The power of money, and its impotence in curing man's unhappiness!

Would he be able to convey his message so everyone could understand him and thereby reduce the sum of suffering? Had he discovered the key to interpreting the age, the bewildering modern world on the eve of the millennium? Could he thereby improve the sad human condition? Or would his quest, his *Pilgrim's Progress*, end in a pilgrim's regress?

Part Two

Voices from the Ganges:

— Buddha showed him the right way.
Will the master's rectification
lead to his edification?

— Can he rectify his direction?
Can he mend his mistakes?
Can he alter his karma?

— Will the quibbler cease to quibble?
Will he turn from dreams to delusion?
Will he lose himself on the way?

Chapter V. A Teacher of the Poor

Before testing his gospel in Manhattan, which many considered the model city of the future and which some regarded as worse than Sodom or Gomorrah, Malunkyaputta rehearsed his message in less developed regions. Anxious to share his tidings, he spoke in Third World countries which most needed his lessons. He spoke wherever he could draw a crowd. He spoke in the slums and marketplaces of Bangladesh, Mexico City, Rio de Janeiro; in Lima, Lesotho, Madagascar. He spoke to the hungry and homeless, the needy and needless, the unemployed fathers of large families, the swollen-bellied mothers of starving children.

Unlike earlier prophets who performed miracles to persuade the people, Malunkyaputta made no extravagant promises and taught nothing but the truth or the facts of life as revealed by Science. To make his sermons more palatable, he'd season them with science-fiction fables, which were his parables. To show his sympathy for the poor and the ignorant, he'd stripped himself of his fine apparel and wore nothing but rags or a loin cloth; at times he'd even preach in the nude. At the end of a session, he'd pass around his begging bowl, for voluntary contributions, which seldom filled the bowl. He journeyed from place to place as best he could, using his old student's passport, hitching a lift on a donkey cart, or riding a borrowed bicycle, or hiding himself as a stowaway on a cruise ship or a jet plane.

Emulating Zarathustra, he spoke fervently in Teheran, exhorting the poor Persians to choose a new style of life as the right way for attaining happiness. Now by this time, factories had been built, even in backward regions, for manufacturing happiness. Shopping malls in Asia and Africa were selling goods that promised unlimited happiness. Satellite stations, circling the global village, broadcast their messages day and night: "Buy what we sell and be happy! We guarantee happiness to everyone! ... Happiness for the greatest number! ... Happiness forever for all! ..."

The celestial advertising tended to confuse the poor.

"Tell me, my deluded people," Malunkyaputta questioned his listeners. "What is your happiness?"

The people told him in diverse tongues: "Happiness is a bowl of rice with a bit of pork... Happiness is a pair of shoes... Happiness is a bicycle... A TV set... A new baby! ... Happiness is to buy what we want from all the goods in the world! ...."

"O my bewildered brothers," said Malunkyaputta with a sigh. "All the goods in the world won't guarantee you happiness! I know, for I was rich once, rich with the world's treasure. You must choose another way. Choose to live by the light of reason." He appealed to their understanding. "I teach you the truth, believe me, the truth revealed by Science, and the truth shall set you free. If you could control your breeding, you'd all have more and more of the goods you crave."

Some of the poor Pakistanis applauded him. "Preach, brother, preach!" they shouted. "Teach us to be free!"

A few tossed small coins in his bowl.

But many were disappointed. "We don't understand you," they said. "Where's all your money gone, mister?"

"Why did you give it away?"

"We want the real goods of the world!"

"We need cake and gin for our happiness..."

(2)

After further testing, Malunkyaputta observed that his gospel was becoming less and less popular in the Third World. No one seemed to understand his message. He decided to transfer his mission to New York and try a fresh approach. New York was the magnet of the world's more ambitious refugees and speculators, still yearning to be free. It furnished a preview of the future. It had more skyscrapers and slums, more grand hotels and soup kitchens, more music halls and noise-makers, more rats and cockroaches than any other city. It was said to offer not only free speech but also unlimited opportunity to every immigrant, regardless of race, color, creed or gender. Some called it the first melting pot of America; others called it the last grand sewer of mankind.

In due time, sailing on a freighter from Puerto Rico, Malunkyaputta reached Ellis Island in the middle of November, shortly before Thanksgiving Day. (This was the year when another surprising visitor, Nikita Khrushchev, chief of Communist Russia, toured the United States and told the American people: "We'll bury you...") A small island in New York harbor, Ellis Island was overshadowed by the Statue of Liberty, a monumental lady with an ever-burning torch. Malunkyaputta reached the end of a long line and stood in front of the Immigration Inspector.

The Inspector was a short swarthy man with copper colored skin. He looked at the newcomer sharply, then consulted his latest regulations. The applicant was obviously a derelict, a bare-footed refugee, hungry, homeless, odorous and nearly naked. He was no doubt an illegal immigrant, thoroughly undesirable, and to be deported promptly to Bangladesh or Patagonia or wherever he came from.

Instead of rejecting him, however, the Inspector drew Malunkyaputta aside and put a friendly arm around his shoulder.

"Welcome to America!" he said with a cryptic smile. (He resembled Padman-Ananda.) "You and I are both Indians, my friend, which means we are both Native Americans. I am happy to adopt you in our much-promising land. Let me explain the facts. When Columbus reached these shores in 1492, he was searching for a passage to India. And when he saw our red-skinned brothers on the beach, he called them Indians. By mistake? No! By prophetic divination! Our people migrated from Asia, the mother of India, more than 40,000 years ago. They came across an old land bridge between Siberia and Alaska. In time, they settled both the Americas, from Ketchikan to Patagonia. All were Indians. The Mayans, the Aztecs, the Amazonians; the Eskimos and Fuegians; the Mohawks, the Sioux, the Apaches, the Choctaws, the Cherokees, the Crows and a hundred other nations — the Pyramid-Builders, the Scalpers, the Lost Tribes of Israel. All were scattered members of one family! We hunted the deer and the buffalo; we tamed the wild horse; we planted corn, tobacco, peyote beans; we studied the stars; we told each other strange fables; worshipped the Great Spirit. And we managed to multiply. So you see, my son, we so-called redskins, the Amerindians are the true and original Americans. This was our homeland long before the end of the last Ice Age. We had settled here long before the white man came. Which reminds me: one of our grandfathers, an Algonkian, sold Manhattan Island to a white man for $24. Go, my son, visit Mr. Rockefeller and give him our bill, a long-overdue account. He owns much of Manhattan and owes more. Give him your tidings and see if he can hear you. Good luck!"

Malunkyaputta thanked the benevolent Inspector who now resembled a great Indian shaman smoking his pipe of brotherhood, peace, and revelations, the smoke from which rose high and merged with the clouds of mist and fog that shrouded the Statue of Liberty. He turned to leave.

"Wait a minute!" said the Inspector. "You'll need something warmer to wear in Manhattan. It's cold here in November —" He opened a locker and removed a few items from his wardrobe. "Take these." He gave the poor immigrant a blanket, a deerskin jacket, a pair of moccasins. He helped him into his new apparel which, in turn, helped to convert the stranger into a Native American.

Again Malunkyaputta thanked the generous Inspector and, after a bit of additional but perfunctory inspection by Customs, by the Declarations, Affirmations, Denials, Delousing and Fumigation Departments, he left Ellis Island to carry on his mission.

(3)

Within sight of the Statue of Liberty, he surveyed the megalopolis. He gazed at the stupefying ring of skyscrapers which fenced the crowded island. He looked at the pullulating harbor which seemed to be full of barges. The barges were loaded with garbage, and many of the bargemen were desperately searching for places in which to dump the refuse. The towns and villages along the Hudson had been rejecting the ever-growing mountains of waste from Manhattan.

A brass plaque on the base of the Statue bore the familiar lines by Emma Lazarus from *The New Colossus*:

> Give me your tired, your poor,
> Your huddled masses yearning to breathe free,
> The wretched refuse of your teeming shore,
> Send these, the homeless, tempest-tossed, to me:
> I lift my lamp beside the golden door!

(Was Emma Lazarus, the hope-filled Zionist sonneteer, a descendant of Lazarus from Bethany who rose from his tomb on the fourth day, bound in bandages and stinking like a fish, after Jesus had called him in a loud voice: "Lazarus, come forth!" Was she related to the poor man Lazarus who found comfort in Abraham's bosom while the rich man suffered the torments of hell? Was she related to Lady Lazarus of London who fell in love with death too soon and died of self-pity? We haven't room enough to pursue her genealogy.)

Malunkyaputta spoke to the garbage-collectors by the wharf, improvising a parable to spice his message. "My bedeviled brothers," he said, "Our much-promising land has become a polluted land! We suffer from the Ten Plagues of Plenty. No matter where we go, something peculiar falls on our heads every day. One day it rains manna, mixed with showers of burning acid. The next day: petrified eggs, as hard as golf balls. The third day: poisonous toads and phosphorescent fish. The fourth day: dead sea gulls dripping with oil. The fifth day: showers of broken bottles and broken needles. The sixth day: synthetic rubies and real rubber condoms. The seventh day: embryos, abortions, pin-headed babies!

"Who can collect the ever-multiplying manna? No one, for there's too much of things putrefying and not enough room for disposing of the waste. And no one knows how to stop the flood or cap our cornucopia. Some call it the Blessing of Enterprise; others call it the Plagues of Abundance. The poor blame the rich, the blacks blame the whites, the young the old, the old the young.

"Some pray for a messiah. 'Teach us to save ourselves from the mounting flood of much and manna,' they cry. 'Teach us how to endure our selves and our unendurable neighbors. Teach us the wisdom we need to cope with the things that are showered upon us day after day! Teach us to cope with Too Much and Not Enough!'

"Wise men have tried to edify the people. 'Pollution is only a part of our problem,' they explain. 'The rain of muck is the result of overpopulation.' Too many people on the planet. The more people the more pollution. The more people the more hunger. The more hunger the more violence. Now the cause of all this is too much sex. Believe me, brothers, if copulation were as hard as algebra, the race would have died out with the dinosaurs. If we could teach the poor to reduce their rage for multiplying, we would reduce pollution, poverty, disease, violence and war.

"Believe me, brothers, this remains our most urgent, and most desperate problem. It remains a necessary lesson yet to be learned!"

"What's he trying to sell us?" a bargeman cried. "Where does he come from?" shouted another. A third one shook his fist. "He sounds un-American!"

(4)

As the kind Inspector had advised him, Malunkyaputta rode the subway to Rockefeller Towers. He emerged from underground and found himself before a cathedral-like structure which rose high above the surrounding cluster of skyscrapers. The entrance was flanked by two enormous bronze statues: one of Prometheus proffering mankind his wand of fire; the other of kneeling Atlas holding the Earth on his shoulders. Malunkyaputta entered a vast lobby and tried to find Mr. Rockefeller's office. He spoke on a free phone in the lobby with Mr. Rockefeller's receptionist who advised him to take the express elevator to the 50th floor.

But the Captain of the Guards kept a sharp eye on the intruder. He refused to admit him into the express elevator. When Malunkyaputta searched for a stairway to the upper regions, the Captain blew his whistle to summon two guards who promptly escorted him to the exit.

Meditating for awhile, Malunkyaputta walked about the fine plaza, west of the Towers, and observed the sightseers. Most of the people seemed well-dressed, well-fed, self-satisfied or somnolent. They strolled in a haze of self-assured prosperity. They seemed to have no burning concern with decalogs or beatitudes. Malunkyaputta remembered how carefully Matthew had arranged the Sermon on the Mount with the Ten Beatitudes as a tableau to match Moses on Sinai with his tablet of the Ten Commandments. Rockefeller Plaza seemed a good place for trying out a sermon.

Emulating Moses, he addressed the crowd: "Open your ears, my friends, I give you a new decalog to fit the times. A few rules to help us save our endangered planet.

- I will honor the living for each belongs to the kingdom of life, and each is related to all.
- I will learn to love my neighbor, with all his faults, as I will learn to love myself, with all my failings.
- I am a part of all my ancestors: I owe myself and my gifts to nameless and numberless multitudes.
- I can free myself from false beliefs and old tyrannies; the tyranny of idols; the tyranny of the many or the few; the tyranny of lies, fears, delusions, greed and desire...
- If the old gods are dead, I can invent a better god.
- If the universe is meaningless, I can invent my own meaning.
- I can pursue the good, the true, and the beautiful, by the light of reason, if I choose. I can also pursue the false, the absurd, or the dreadful, if that is my choice.
- I respect everyone's rights to freedom of choice; free speech; and all human rights... I uphold my right to unpolluted air; an uncongested earth; and uncontested privacy.
- To change the planet's future, I first must change myself.
- If I can change my own tomorrow, I may change all my neighbors' tomorrows... Honor your tomorrow: it may be a new world's Sabbath..."

Some of the sightseers laughed at the simple-minded street preacher. Some gawked at him. They had met on the Plaza in the middle of the 20th century. Why were they there, at that particular point in space and time? No one knew why. Yet their meeting was as predetermined as the trajectory of Halley's or Shoemaker Levy's comet.

— "Who does he think he is?"

— "Another Messiah?"

— "Where does he get such high-falutin' notions?"

— "I've a right to hate my neighbor, as much as Mr. Rockefeller, haven't I?"

Some dropped bills in his bowl and hurried away.

"Wait, friends, don't leave me," said Malunkyaputta. "Listen to my Beatitudes!"

Emulating the Galilean, he recited after Matthew:

"Blessed are the poor who refrain from multiplying.
Blessed are the barren who refrain from crowding the city.
Blessed are the meek who refrain from adding new mouths
    to the dugs of Starvation.
Blessed are the mindful who choose not to multiply.
Blessed are the needy who refrain from polluting the
    New Jerusalem.
Blessed are the hungry, for they shall be replenished.
Blessed are the mournful, for they shall be entertained.
Blessed are the peacemakers, for they shall be promoted.
Blessed are the persecuted, for they shall be rewarded.
Blessed are the rich, for they shall be transported..."

By this time the crowd in the Plaza was becoming hostile. "He sounds too democratic!" shouted one. "A goddam red!" cried another. An indignant broker from Westchester reported him as a public nuisance. Mr. Rockefeller himself looked out the window of his office on the fiftieth floor and pressed the buzzer for his Receptionist. Then the Captain of the Guards appeared below, blowing his whistle, followed by four burly guards. They surrounded the trouble-maker. He struggled with them. They beat him with their batons and bloodied his face. They knocked him to the ground. Then a van pulled up to cart him away to the nearby police station.

In a little while the Receptionist came to the station to bail him out. "Mr. Rockefeller's orders," she said, and they let him go.

Malunkyaputta wanted to thank her. The Receptionist was an efficient harridan who resembled Our Precious Lady Stepmother, familiar to him from a former life. But he lost her in the crowd of shoppers on Fifth Avenue. The shops were elegant and crammed with all sorts of treasures, and many of the shoppers were beautiful young women with elusive smiles. He wandered down Broadway to Fourteenth Street and Union Square and passed through East Village. For awhile he seemed to be following a beautiful nurse in a white uniform who reminded him of Mia.

The nurse was leading him toward Brooklyn Bridge.

Late on a cold windy afternoon, a day before Thanksgiving, Malunkyaputta reached the Bowery, a grim and forsaken district. In Peter Stuyvesant's time, three centuries earlier, it had been a flourishing Dutch farm in a garden-like valley called the Bouwerij. Now it was a slum, lined with abandoned tenements and fire-gutted warehouses, cheap hotels and saloons. Acres of the wide westward sloping pavement had become a camping ground for hundreds and hundreds of homeless and hungry people. They lay on the stone pavement in a stupor or huddled in the doorways of the abandoned tenements.

On a rise of land in the southeast corner stood a Soup Kitchen, next to a small church — God's True Chapel, where an invisible preacher was rehearsing a group of hymn-singers. The Chapel stood near a long rectangular building, the Free Clinic, where a line of pregnant girls was awaiting admission by a pair of physicians in white lab coats and their volunteer nurses. To the southeast lay Canal Street, Chinatown, and a maze of stone alleys which led to the waterfront. Above it rose the monumental arches of Brooklyn Bridge.

The ghost of Walt Whitman seemed to be looming over the bridge. The poet-prophet had often crossed the bay by the Brooklyn Ferry. He had strolled for years up and down Broadway, celebrating himself, celebrating million-footed Manhattan, and celebrating the ever-expanding States. He had catalogued the wonders of America. He had witnessed the Civil War, led by Lincoln to abolish human slavery. Bard of the average and divine Everyman, he had praised America as the greatest of nations. Promoting his vision of universal democracy, he had embraced all mankind in his democratic arms.

He seemed to be welcoming Malunkyaputta in his prophetic *Passage to India*: "You too I welcome fully the same as the rest... The earth to be spanned, connected by network... The lands to be welded together... Down from the gardens of Asia descending, radiating, Adam and Eve appear, then their myriad progeny after them... Europe to Asia, Africa joined, and they to the New World... The streams of the Indus and the Ganges and their many affluents... I, my shores of America walking today, behold, resuming all. Old occult Brahma. The tender and junior Buddha...

"Passage to more than India! Are thy wings plumed indeed for such far flights? Soundest below the Sanskrit and the Vedas? Sail forth! Steer for deep waters only... We are bound where mariner has not yet dared to go... The seas all crossed, weathered the capes, the voyage done... Filled with friendship, love complete, the Elder Brother found, the Younger melts in fondness in his arms..."

Malunkyaputta took up his station by the Soup Kitchen and surveyed the congregation of derelicts in front of him. He had set out on a mission to teach the poor; and here were his students, his school, his academy and arena. The people on the pavement were among the poorest of the poor. The refuse of Manhattan. Unskilled, unemployable, diseased or demented, they were part of a surplus population. Some existed on welfare; some survived on public or private charity. Pariahs or parasites, many were slaves to their poverty, their sloth or greed or ignorance.

Heirs of Walt Whitman, each was his own poet. Each had universal cravings. Each was composing a song of himself or celebrating America with psalms of praise or malediction. Their forefathers had escaped to freedom from Europe, Asia, or Africa. They wore in their much-tried bodies the marks of a new world; its mountains, plains, and rivers; its history and geography, North, East, South, and West; its bloody strikes and uprisings, revolutions, civil wars, and wars abroad.

Plato saw two cities in Athens: the City of the Rich and the City of the Poor. The same was true of nearly all the world's ever more congested cities. The people in the Bowery resembled the people Buddha saw by the Ganges. They resembled the people in Dante's Purgatory. "The poor are always with us," Jesus observed.

Could Malunkyaputta reach them with his message? Could he teach them the power of man's reason to choose a new direction and cure the cause of human suffering?

*　*　*

A homeless man carrying a mug of hot coffee from the Soup Kitchen passed by Malunkyaputta and, noticing his evangelical air, winked at him encouragingly: "Preach, Brother, preach! Tell us all about God. Teach us the truth if you dare..."

"I teach only the truth," said Malunkyaputta. Yet what could he tell them about God that was both true and self-evident? Like

51

Buddha, he had no traffic with the supernatural or the anthropomorphic gods of the priests. Yet man was a god-craving god-making, god-destroying animal, with ambitions perhaps to become a god himself. Aristotle's God was the First Mover or Prime Cause. Spinoza's God was Nature. If a triangle could think, he said, it would think that God was a Cosmic Triangle. Poor Jesus thought God was his Benevolent Father and considered himself God's own Beloved Son.

Malunkyaputta raised his voice above the hymn-singers in God's True Chapel, the mission next to the Soup Kitchen, and gave the glum crowd in the Bowery another version of his gospel. While he was speaking, hordes of feral children were rummaging in garbage cans in the dark alleys south of the Bowery and their cries could be heard: "Why are we so many? … Why's there no room for us? … Why are we always hungry?" And their cries seemed to blend with the hoarse rumbling voices of men on the pavement: "Too many mouths, not enough bread… Too many hands, not enough jobs… Too many bottles, not enough gin…"

"In the beginning, my friends, God was a blunderer," Malunkyaputta launched his sermon. "Working by trial and error, he made millions of mistakes. But in time, our blundering beginner improved. Ten billion years or so after the first Big Bang, he produced not only clouds of galaxies and deep black holes, he also begot green plants and worms to fertilize our planet, Terra Firma. In time, he produced Adam, an apprentice god in a way, but also a blunderer. We're all the children of Adam, to be sure, ever-multiplying and ever-blundering. Our Father Adam cavorting in the hot jungles of Eden, east of Madagascar, begot a large progeny. To tell the truth my friends, our ancestors were apes. We mustn't forget the plain scientific fact: no matter how far we may have advanced in the last million years, we remain close to the chimps. But we also can learn from Father Adam's mistakes. We have acquired the power of reason and the power of choice. To have room and food and good things for everyone, we can choose to control our breeding by the light of reason.   We can choose to breed out the worst and breed for the best.   If we choose to control our breeding—"

"Control our breathing, he says?" cried a derelict from Nashville, Tennessee. "What next? The air's foul enough, to be sure, but we'd die without air!" Another heckler cried: "Tain't lawful to be preachin' evolution!"

Malunkyaputta tried to explain what he meant. He was interrupted by a sudden commotion. A crowd of angry demonstrators was marching into the Bowery from behind God's True Chapel. Carrying banners and posters, singing hymns or shouting slogans, they were demonstrating against the Birth Control Clinic next to the mission. The posters showed aborted fetuses dripping with ketchup and a tangle of dead baby baboons.

"Defend the unborn!" the protesters were shouting.

"Wage a holy war! Join our crusade! Burn down the devil's clinics! Avenge a million dead babies! Kill the abortion doctors!"

Others shouted slogans with patriotic fervor:

"Rescue America! We must have godly laws in our land again! Hang the baby-killers! Save the Mother of God! — An eye for an eye, in Jesus' name! — We're in a war! Save America!"

The rioters were preparing to storm the clinic. Listening to their angry voices, Malunkyaputta felt that many of the protestors were pious people who believed in the sanctity of life, and he sympathized with their belief. Yet he also knew that they were ignorant and irrational. Unwanted children were a chief source of human suffering. They bred hunger, poverty, pollution, more and more violence and war.

While the protestors were surrounding the clinic, the preacher slipped out of God's True Chapel. He had pulled a black ski-mask over his face and was carrying a duffel bag. Approaching the entrance to the clinic, he zipped open the bag and removed a rifle. He half-knelt, took aim, and started to fire. He shot and killed the two doctors and wounded the nurses. When Malunkyaputta moved to disarm him, the preacher turned on him and shot him in the left shoulder. While Malunkyaputta fell to the pavement, the terrorist turned again and, pushing his way through the turbulent crowd, fled from the scene.

Meanwhile, a formidable policewoman on horseback had appeared. Trying to quell the riot, the Police Captain fired a signal gun and spoke into her walkie-talkie to summon reinforcements. An ambulance came, with wailing sirens, followed by a mobile TV crew. The crew filmed the storming of the clinic by the demonstrators and the shooting of the doctors and nurses by the masked preacher. Simultaneously, scenes from the riot in the Bowery began to appear on TV sets throughout Manhattan, then throughout the world. The same scenes were mirrored in a battered set by the Soup Kitchen.

A cryptically smiling young woman, the chief TV commentator in New York, was analyzing the news:

"The attack on the clinic in the Bowery is similar to recent attacks on clinics in Boston, Chicago, Los Angeles; Dallas, Atlanta, San Diego; Tallahassee, Pensacola... The violent demonstrators appear to be well-organized... Are they supported by a network of terrorists? ... Is this part of a national conspiracy?

"Stay tuned to your station, please, Your Window on the World. Moment by moment, we bring before your eyes what's happening, as it is happening, so you may witness the truth and terror of our times. Acts of random violence! The homeless and hungry dying in the street! ... The masked preacher with the rifle! ... Volunteer doctors and nurses, gunned down in the hospital! ..."

The TV Commentator presented flash interviews, one after another, in rapid-fire tempo. "Our civic leaders—" she cried, unveiling a gallery of gargoyles.

Mayor Hogan: "The violence must end! ... We call on the police to guard all the clinics."

Governor Brooks: "We are alerting the state troopers..."

The Attorney General: "The Justice Department is dispatching federal marshals with 2000 deputies to protect 1500 clinics..."

"A reward is posted—" Donor Munger: "Planned Parenthood Foundation is offering $100,000 for information leading to the capture and conviction of the terrorist..."

Detective Hotchkiss: "We have traced the rifle to a gunshop in Salem, New Hampshire..."

FBI Agent 606: "We now suspect that the fugitive preacher is an unemployed barber from Boston..."

High churchmen. Bishop Brogan: "We deplore the violence. We call for a halt to the vigils and demonstrations... We must revise our strategy..." Cardinal Kelly: "We are cancelling our plans to hold an anti-abortion mass on Thanksgiving Day..."

A voice from the White House: The President: "Violence must end...We condemn this form of domestic terrorism... The right to free choice is every woman's right..."

A pundit from Harvard, Professor Morton, a controversial biologist: "What's behind the attacks on the clinics? Who benefits from the new planetary plague, the spreading infection, the uncontrolled breeding of more and more idiots? Look to the religious fanatics. The patriots who want bigger armies. The arms dealers and war makers. The businessmen who want more consumers. The astronauts, plotting to colonize Mars…"

The TV Commentator concluded her analysis: "Stay tuned to us, please. We are your Window on the World. Moment by moment, we bring before your eyes what's happening, as it is happening, so you may witness the truth and terror of our times and judge for yourself the living history of the hour!"

The program closed with a view of Malunkyaputta on a stretcher in an ambulance which sped away with shrieking sirens toward the Manhattan Asylum for the mad.

*   *   *

Three shadowy figures gazed after the ambulance from a ramp of Brooklyn Bridge on a gray-black dawn hour.

The policewoman on horseback who may have been Our Precious Lady Stepmother, said: "Is this then the end of our experiment?"

"No," said the preacher with the rifle who resembled Padman-Ananda. "He must continue his quest, for he has yet to find the right way."

The beautiful nurse in white whispered: "Will he find the right way in an asylum for the mad?"

Chapter VI. The Missionary

On the way to the hospital the ambulance ran into a garbage truck on Lexington Avenue near East 48th Street. The crash forced open the rear door of the ambulance and flung Malunkyaputta out onto the pavement like a sack of stones. The paramedics picked him up and rushed him to the emergency room of the asylum. In addition to his bullet wounds, he had broken ribs, broken arms and legs, a broken spine, among other thorns in the flesh.

At first, the physicians refused to treat him. He was obviously a basket case, a welfare client, a foreigner. "Beyond repair," said an intern. "Not worth the time," said a specialist. "Hopeless," said the resident. Then, rising to the challenge, they decided to apply the latest resources of medical science to salvage him. In the next six months they sutured nearly every inch of his body and replaced his spine with an aluminum frame. They filled him with fresh blood through intravenous tubes and fed him plasma to serve as his soma. They strengthened his heart with a platinum pacemaker. They gouged out his myopic eye-balls and replaced them with bright plastic lenses which gave him double vision. They treated him with powerful experimental drugs, chemotherapy, electric shocks, laughing gas. In effect, they resurrected him.

During his convalescence in the Asylum, he suffered from occasional spells of amnesia or deja vu. He recalled fragments from his former lives and spoke with his familiars from the ashram. Sometimes he stuttered; sometimes he spoke in tongues. Psychiatrists visited him and listened to his feverish rambling.

"The scales have fallen from my eyes," declared Malunkyaputta. "I see the light ahead... I am the Alpha, and also the Omega... I am the way to revelations... I will unriddle the last mysteries... I will become all things to all men, or no thing to no man... I have passed beyond the road to Damascus..."

"He suffers from delusions," observed one psychiatrist.

"Grandiosity," said another.

"Alienation," judged a third. "Out of touch with the real world, he remains an incurable."

The day came when Malunkyaputta was discharged from the Asylum. A bionic man, fitted with new eyes, a new heart, and other improvements, he was free to pursue his karma in the jungles of Manhattan. Still shrouded in gauze bandages, he resembled an Egyptian mummy or a visitor from Mars. A lean and singular figure, he had a rapt and increasingly prophetic air.

Despite his otherworldly appearance, he was eager to resume preaching his gospel, which he preached even more fervently than before. Science was the application of reason to man's problems, and reason was man's highest faculty. Science could cure mankind's ailments; it could free men of pain, fear, confusion, suffering, unhappiness. Science could turn the Earth into Everyman's Edengarden; it held the keys to the kingdom of God.

Pursuing his missionary labors, he preached his gospel on the steps in front of the Grand Cathedral of Saint John the Divine, till the police interrupted him. He preached it on the street corners in a dozen crowded cities along the East Coast and again reciting the Scientist's Credo:

1. I will pursue the truth behind the mystery of things and, by understanding the laws of nature, to penetrate the secrets of creation or the Mind of God.
2. I will strive to preserve the Earth, without fear or favor; to keep its waters, air and soil free of pollution; to save its plants and animals, its forests and the tree of life.
3. I will strive to add to all men's freedom. Freedom from poverty, ignorance, disease. Freedom from overcrowding. Freedom from pollution. Freedom from falsehood. Freedom from the fear of death...

Malunkyaputta described his view of a New Eden: Earth's population is limited by voluntary planning. Instead of ten billion crowded inhabitants, a global population of ten million or less is the norm. Poverty, hunger, disease, and ignorance are abolished. The breeding of the best human stock becomes everyman's ideal. Though men are few, they are free and each person has new worth and dignity in his fellowmen's eyes. Every man, woman, and child is wanted and needed. Every child is welcomed as a natural miracle. Each has a chance to develop his talents to its highest potential.

Wilderness regions develop as mankind's chosen habitat. A few planned capital cities are built for beauty, splendor, and magnificence. Men enjoy both privacy and community. They meet for games and great festivals; they celebrate the brotherhood of man; they take delight in each other's company.

Instead of brute competition and rivalry, men practice mature aid for the enhancement of life. Instead of cutting each other's throats, they cultivate manners, morals, mindfulness; taste, style, character. Each in his own person seeks to raise evolving mankind to higher states of awareness, grace, understanding. This will nurture a new kind of man: It will mean a great forward leap for humanity.

In this new order, Malunkyaputta promised, all men will have a chance to develop their highest powers: Each may become an athlete, an artist, a scientist, a philosopher. Each may be noble, courageous, wise, free, kind, creative, compassionate and magnanimous.

"This means a great new stage in the evolution of humanity," Malunkyaputta promised.

Despite his eloquence, his gospel did not draw many converts. His bowl was seldom filled; his feet were bare. Meanwhile, his rival evangelists, who preached their lurid lies of hell-fire and damnation, could launch crusades which drew millions of pious followers. They acquired radio or TV stations, built cathedrals, brainwashed the young, established foundations and Swiss bank accounts.

It was all mystifying. What sort of a world was he living in? Who were his neighbors? Who were their leaders? Whither was America bound? What was real, what was illusory? How could he edify himself?

A mystery lay hidden below the flux of things, and Malunkyaputta hoped to penetrate it. He wanted to understand himself, his neighbors, and the world. He craved to decipher the sign of his times, for better or worse.

*   *   *

While pursuing his mission, Malunkyaputta sought to fathom the paradoxical Americans.

A nation of nations, they came from all parts of the earth, from the heartland of England, Scotland, and Ireland, the ghettos of Europe, the slums of Asia and Africa. They were remarkably greedy and generous, shrewd and gullible, pious and violent. They could learn the best of the past, yet many remained unteachable. They invented thousands of useful gadgets, along with the most dangerous devices. They could talk around the world but could not communicate with their neighbors. They had more freedom than they could use or knew what to do with. They could rule the world but would not rule themselves. Free to vote for the best and the brightest, they often gave power to the glibbest demagogue. They spent billions on education, and more billions on building deadly weapons. They celebrated the blessings of democracy, but lived in a state of anarchy. Though they were guaranteed a bill of rights — "life, liberty, and the pursuit of happiness" — many preferred the pursuit of death and bondage and unhappiness. They built huge atomic power plants, but didn't know where to dump the lethal waste. A most prosperous colony of mankind, they built more schools, churches, hospitals, insane asylums and jails than any other people on earth...

By and large, they had faith in applied science. Whether it was a bottomless cornucopia of goods and pleasures or a new Pandora's box of afflictions was not their concern. The gurus of science had produced the mushroom clouds over the rubble of Hiroshima: they were the makers of man's most destructive power... A rival priesthood, Russian scientists had launched the Sputnik, a satellite which transported a noted dog named Laika; they sent Yuri Gagarin, the first man into space in 1961...

*   *   *

A missionary for peace and the brotherhood of man, Malunkyaputta tried to interpret the events he witnessed between 1960 and 1976.

The Cuban missile crisis seemed to herald an apocalyptic age. Everyone who survived the second half of the 20th century, which some have called the most horrible century of all time, knows about the missile crisis. The brute facts have been recounted in hundreds of memoirs and histories. The confrontation between America and Russia took place within a few short weeks in the fall of 1961.

By this time, Fidel Castro had become dictator of Cuba, a sugar island less than a hundred miles from Florida. Castro had formed a pact with his sponsor, Nikita Khrushchev, the leader of

Communist Russia, who secretly shipped and installed a ring of nuclear missiles on Cuba. The new elected American president, John Kennedy first sought to topple Castro by invading Cuba, but the Bay of Pigs invasion turned into a fiasco. After much debate with his advisors, Kennedy put the nation's armed forces on maximum alert and issued an ultimatum to Khrushchev, in effect: "Remove the missiles, or else—" The world was on the brink of a nuclear holocaust. Kennedy's brother, the Attorney General, estimated "60 million Americans killed and as many Russians, or more." Khrushchev, who had miscalculated Kennedy's resolution, warned his own generals of the prospect: "the death of 500 million human beings." To avoid a thermo-nuclear exchange, he agreed to dismantle the missiles in Cuba. An aide in the White House praised Kennedy: "He has guts. He has guts...We were eyeball to eyeball, and they blinked."

Malunkyaputta was disturbed. Were the majority of people merely pawns in their leaders' game of power? How could they let them gamble so recklessly with millions of lives? And what could Malunkyaputta do about it? He was a zero in an endless string of zeros, at the mercy of the new magi, the physicists, the Fates.

A jingle occurred to him:

> "What makes me so clever?" asked Doktor Heller,
> pater of the hell-bomb, standing tall.
> "Because of all the queer birds on Earth,
> I'm the queerest duck of them all!"

To register his protest, Malunkyaputta drafted a petition:

"We the living who desire not to die, surprised by radiant fire hurled without warning from the depths of space by robot rocketeers; we who would voyage with our fellows on earth, nor fear the innocent skies, address the ambassadors of the divided house and their overlords in the chambers of power:

"Masters of those who know the secret of secrets, guardians of good and evil, do not divide the atom to give each of the living a fragmentary death; divide it so each may inherit a portion of life sweeter than any yet known; divide it so each may share the good news of a common earth and sky...

"Open the doors of our tombs today, open our doors to tomorrow, before the eyeless are stoned by the blind: Do not deny our petition. Let this petition be signed by the young and the old in all our doomed towns and villages; let our voices be heard in the chambers of power, and in the darkening chambers of each man's heart…"

He sent copies of his petition to all the ambassadors of the United Nations; to movers and shakers in Washington, Moscow, Havana, Cambridge, Bombay, New Delhi, Mecca, Jerusalem, the Vatican, and even remoter places. He sent copies to deans of colleges, charitable foundations, international religious orders and poetry societies, hoping they might translate his petition into diverse languages, including Greek, Latin, Hebrew, Sanskrit and Esperanto or Volapuk. Though he spent much on postage, he received no response, except the dignified response of silence or, occasionally, a few negligible requests for donations. In due time, he did receive a visit from an FBI agent who warned him that it was dangerous for a private citizen to harass public officials or meddle with affairs of state.

$$* \quad * \quad *$$

The Cuban missile crisis ended, but the cold war and the arms race continued and escalated.

To contain the spread of communism, President Kennedy sent troops into Vietnam, a province in Indo-China, 10,000 miles west of San Francisco. The campaign in the jungles of Asia turned into a quagmire. In the long disastrous years that followed, the war in Vietnam became America's most unpopular war.

The crusade in the jungles abroad was protested by violent upheavals at home. It was marked by bloody riots, the burning of cities, assassinations; looting and corruption; a rise in cynicism or apathy; a decline in public morality. Almost any almanac of the times, between 1960 and 1976, will furnish a sampler of the facts.

In 1960, an estimated 8 million Americans watched the TV debates between presidential candidates John Kennedy and Richard Nixon… In 1961, departing President Eisenhower warned the country against the growing influence of the military-industrial complex. In 1962, the first black student was admitted to the University of Mississippi, after 3000 federal troops stopped local riots… Governor Wallace of Alabama declared: "I say segregation now, segregation tomorrow, segregation forever." In 1963, some 200,000 persons demonstrated in Washington in support of black demands for civil rights… In 1963, President Kennedy was assassinated in Dallas, Texas… In 1964, Congress passed civil rights bill to ban all discrimination against blacks... In 1965, Malcolm X was shot to death... In 1965, blacks in Watts rioted, burning down the ghetto and looting Los Angeles... (In 1966-67, similar riots broke out in the ghettos of Newark, New Jersey and Detroit, Michigan.) In 1968, Martin Luther King was assassinated in Memphis, Tennessee... In 1968, presidential candidate Robert Kennedy was shot to death in Los Angeles... In 1969, some 250,000 marched in Washington, protesting the war in Vietnam... In 1970, protesting students at Kent State University, Ohio, were shot and killed by National Guardsmen. Protest riots spread to 450 college campuses. In May 1972, Governor Wallace of Alabama, campaigning for the presidency, was shot. In 1972, five men were arrested for breaking into Democratic party headquarters in Washington... In 1973, top Nixon aides, including his chief of staff and the attorney general, were found guilty of obstructing justice and were sentenced to prison... In 1974, President Nixon, faced with impeachment for abuses of power, resigned... In 1975, Vietnam War ended, with occupation of South Vietnam by Communist troops...

The war had cost the lives of 1.2 million persons... Since 1961, it had cost the U.S. alone $28 million per day. In May, 1975, Congress voted $405 million in aid to South Vietnamese refugees, of whom 140,000 were flown to the U.S.... So the American people paid for the blunders and deceit of their leaders.

*   *   *

Malunkyaputta tried to make out the hidden design behind the ever-multiplying facts. Did they portend the decline of the American Republic? Did the noble Greeks or Romans suspect that they were declining or degenerating? Who could say? Thousands of facts and rumors poured from the press: reports of riots and civil wars, assassinations, acts of terror and treachery. (Similar facts had been known to Thucydides, Tacitus, Gibbon, each of whom traced the decline of a great empire.)

He tried to understand the paradoxical world he lived in. He was perplexed by the enormous war budgets and the perpetual preparation for war. The lewd feud of each against all; the old war of all against all. He tried to understand the crusade against communism. Was it a war of the "haves" against the "have-nots"; the rich against the poor? The war of civilized people against the barbarians that threatened its frontier? Rousseau, a herald of the French Revolution, observed: "Man is born free, yet everywhere he's in chains..." Marx proclaimed in his manifesto: "Workers of the world, unite! You have nothing to lose but your chains! ..." America was a Christian nation. The early Christians shared their goods and tried to love each other in the name of Jesus. Communism was, in effect, a form of primitive Christianity. Yet, in the name of liberating and loving their fellows, communism had enslaved and reduced them. Jesus, Marx, Lenin, Stalin, Hitler, Mao — all were, in a sense, messiahs or rival messiahs or social engineers. Stalin, determined to industrialize feudal Russia, liquidated millions of farmers. Hitler, promoting a master race, raised Auschwitz for his monument. Mao, a disciple of Lenin, led nearly a billion people in China into a Communist Utopia or dystopia. All were messiahs or rival messiahs.

*   *   *

An astonishing event took place on July 20, 1969, when Neil Armstrong became the first man to walk on the Moon. "One small step for man," said Armstrong. "A giant leap for mankind." Malunkyaputta meditated on the remarkable performance. He viewed the future with mixed feelings:

Man in Orbit

Behold what comes forth out of mud to cast
        his moving shadow across a web of stars:
A question-mark from the deepest well of time
        that spirals from the ameba toward the moon.

In fear and trembling at first, but ever more boldly
        He leaves the ooze of his puddles and rises to soar,
To girdle the globe, to race beyond the earth,
        to measure his tomb while planets await his call.

Confounder of reason, compounded of paradox:
        In fear of his fellows he sails his end-earth weapon,
        In love of his fellows, he burns himself for fuel:
Himself the arrow-in-flight and the target-in-place!
        A thinking atom: the riddle in the rocket,
        composed of elements old as the oldest star.

63

* * *

Malunkyaputta pursued his mission in a turbulent land. In
addition to preaching his gospel, he took part in marches and
demonstrations, from Selma, Mississippi to Boston, Massachusetts.
Although he resembled a noble Hindu prince in exile, people in the
South called him Nigger Boy. In Alabama, he was sprayed with tear
gas by the police; in Georgia, they threatened him with the chain
gang. He was repeatedly arrested, examined and cross-examined,
reprimanded, fined or jailed in towns and villages with resonant
names such as Antioch, Corinth, Jericho; Troy, Babylon, Rome,
Philadelphia... Like the missionary he was emulating,
Malunkyaputta was often beaten or bludgeoned. He was in danger
from rising rivers and floods, danger from muggers, danger in the
city, danger in the wilderness, danger from false brothers. He was
often hungry and thirsty, often cold and homeless.

At this time, he felt a bond with the blacks; while in jail in
Memphis, Tennessee, he composed *A Black Boy's Songs* to convey
his feelings:

(1)

Caliban's Cry
When I walked abroad in my birthday suit,
black from the suns of Africa,
they trapped me in a net of thorns
and locked me in a silent cell.

When I tried to sing a brave new song,
I shook with Caliban's awful cries:
they pulled out my tongue to stop the noise
and left me with a muted mouth.

(2)

The Lord Is My Hunter
Their Lord is my Hunter, I am his prey:
He tracks me down wherever I may hide.

He searches me out with measuring eyes,
He bars my path with his net of thorns.

He poisons our pastures, pollutes our waters;
He blinds us with hunger and thirst.

All the days of my life he pursues me —
Their Lord is my Hunter: I am his prey…

(3)

The Sea Wind's Promise
A black boy runs in burning shoes
    in a wilderness of grief;
All the signs he reads are riddles,
    all the turns he takes are wrong…

Lie down, cries the wind to the black boy,
    Our breath will blow you seaward.
Lie down, roars the sea, lie down:
    Our tides will wash you clean.
Lie down, sing the moon and the stars,
    Our beams will lighten your heart.
Lie down, sing the tides, lie down:
    Our foam will whiten your bones.

We'll spread your atoms equally
    Through democratic time and change.
Lie down and let the winds and tides
    Restore you to the universe.

*   *   *

He also composed a tribute to Martin Luther King who had
recently been shot down in Memphis:

In Memoriam
(Martin Luther King)

A black man in our town of gray despair,
he walked unarmed among his enemies.
A brave man in our streets of hidden fear,
he led his people in the march for peace.

A bold man in our time of rage and terror,
he made the brotherhood of man his creed.
A seeker in our thorny fields of error,
he cast himself among the thorns for seed.

65

A fearful white man felled him in our day,
as any Cain might strike down a bold reaper.
As any Cain who'd mask his act, we say:
"No fault of mine. Am I my brother's keeper?"
Whose martyred blood will quench the flames of hate
incandescent in our darkening state?

*   *   *

The scene was confusing. More and more often, Malunkyaputta observed signs of decay in America. By the spring of 1975 a continental smog had spread over the land and its people. Cynicism, greed, violence, escape into drugs and sex formed a part of it. A stench was permeating the air. A pungent odor, like burnt rubber; a fetid fecal stink, like formaldehyde; a sweet and bitter smell of corruption.

Great cities, ringed with skyscrapers, were falling into ruins, surrounded by slums and ghettos and burnt-out tenements. Noise-makers multiplied; schools and courts were turning into towers of Babel; professors spoke in techno-babble, jargon, or gibberish. They published book after book on the new culture, biology, physics or metaphysics, which added to collective delusions. New Age cults were popular, along with acts of terrorism. Millions of computers were spinning a world-web of misinformation or trivia for millions of new breeders, consumers and polluters in the techno-ghettos of cyberspace. Democracy was degenerating into a circus, a global theatre of absurdity.

Seething with resentment, confused and frustrated, thousands of students were rioting in colleges across the country, from Boston to Berkeley. They occupied administrative offices and attacked their professors, who became adept in appeasing the barbarians.

Flower Children appeared, wearing bluejeans, T-shirts, rags, saffron robes, leather jackets or other fantastic costumes. Some 300,000 were drifting through the towns and cities of America. They grew long hair, the boys resembled girls, some shaved their skulls. They floated in a haze of marijuana, coke, LSD. Children of prosperous citizens pretended to be homeless and hungry and panhandled in the streets. Some were runaways and became teenage hustlers and prostitutes, drug-peddlers, AIDS carriers. Some played the guitar, sang gospel hymns or chanted Hare Krishna; some joined the Nation of Islam. Black or white, they believed it was cool to sleep in abandoned buildings, hostels, parks or jungles. They re-named themselves as they chose and called each other by code names: Rag Doll, Bambi, Coyote, Worm; Catfish, Misty, Dracula; Skywalker, Loaded, Butterfly, Skunk; Crappy, Shaggy, Moondrop, Star-Monkey, et cetera....

* * *

Malunkyaputta visited Cambridge in April 1975. On a Sunday afternoon he preached to a group of Flower Children who were camping by the banks of the Charles River absorbed in their dream world.

He launched his gospel of science by reciting his *Children's Credo*: "I was born on the Earth because I was wanted. I deserve to be cherished, nourished, preserved, and encouraged. I was born to walk upright and inherit the stars... I will learn from all things, and teach myself freedom from fear. I can speak the truth; I will sing and dance the truth... I will share the truth with my fellows, as I would share the Earth with all the living. As a poet observed, 'I am a man, so nothing human is alien to me.' Nor is any living thing an alien to me... Though one among many, where many may be muted, I was born with a mouth that can speak the words of choice and understanding: I can choose to say yes or no in every hour of my life. 'Yes!' to Goodness, Truth, and Beauty. 'Yes!' to Justice and Freedom. 'No!' to Cruelty and ugliness. 'No!' to Pretension or Falsehood; Ignorance, Disease, and Fear..."

The Flower Children gazed at him with blank or hostile faces.

Malunkyaputta continued his sermon.

"Let me tell you a little science-fiction story," he said, trying to entertain them. *"The Paragon of Paragons..."*

"Hoping to breed a better type of mankind, a team of biologists tried to produce a model of the superman, American style. They combined and recombined the genes of the more promising specimens: Leonardo, Mozart, Jefferson, Darwin; Edison, Einstein — you may add your own selection. Before long, however, they halted their experiment and considered its possible effects. If the planet were inhabited by prodigies only, each in search of a public, each determined to promote his own work at the expense of his rival: would this not convert the Earth into a state of confusion and intolerable anarchy?" Malunkyaputta smiled and remarked: "From this we may deduce that scientists are not always infallible. In addition to their pretended omniscience, scientists may need to practice the older virtues: moderation, foresight, courage, compassion, and common sense.

"We have faith in science, of course, in man's reason lies our last best hope. But social engineering can become a dangerous game. Technology or drug therapy may not be the way to harmony and happiness. We need something more. Don't you agree?"

The Flower Children stared at him suspiciously. They were bored and puzzled by his preachings.

"Let me try another fable," said Malunkyaputta. *"A Visitor from Betelgeuse..."*

"A noted physicist described mankind as 'an advanced breed of monkeys.' This provoked debates on talk shows, which were relayed to all parts of the globe. Then, a radio message reported the long-anticipated yet incredible news: an alien from outer space was about to visit the Earth to review man's accomplishments. In response, a committee was appointed to select the best examples of homo sapiens. The committee assembled a wax-work exhibit of representative men and their works. They displayed the tableau on a pedestal in front of the World Parliament in Geneva.

"In due time the visitor from Betelgeuse arrived. His arrival went nearly unnoticed, for his space ship was a small transparent metallic ball, smaller than a tennis ball; and the visitor himself resembled a diamond-encrusted stick pin, scintillating with points of prismatic light, but otherwise unremarkable.

"The figures he saw in the tableau through his alien eyes were bearded or naked figures, some holding books or rolls of parchment in their hands, their expressions lofty, resigned, or reproachful. They were offering their best works to posterity: *The Republic, The Divine Comedy, The Ninth Symphony,* and so forth.

"The visitor gazed at the tableau for a moment. He duplicated the figures and their works on a microdot, to be filed in his space ship. 'Curious specimens,' he remarked. 'The species may merit more attention. They're not altogether hopeless.' With that he left the minor planet, returning to Betelgeuse on a beam that moved him faster than the speed of light..."

The Flower Children stared at Malunkyaputta with stony eyes.

"Not altogether hopeless," he repeated to himself. He searched for a way to reach them. He remembered that they were within a stone's throw of M.I.T., the birthplace of computer science. Its father, Norbert Wiener, a mathematician and philosopher, was in effect the prophet of a new age; a computer story might appeal to the Flower Children.

"Another fable," said Malunkyaputta. *"Yah and the Super-Computer."*

"A master of computer science, Professor Yah had spent a lifetime in the laboratory perfecting his model of Ultimo-11. Now he was ready to test it. A white-bearded gentleman in a long white laboratory coat, he was rumored to spend endless hours in meditation inside his private office next to the laboratory; some technicians thought he was communing with the infinite; others said he was fast asleep. His door was marked 'Private' and no one except Professor Yah was ever allowed to enter it.

"On the morning of the test, Professor Yah gazed at his super-computer with awe. He pondered what questions he might put to it. Its capacities were truly prodigious. He had fed it all the accumulated data of science, philosophy, religion; tapes of bibles, scriptures, revelations, along with every fact and formula accrued since the age of Pythagoras. After some reflection, Yah put his leading question in three parts:

1. Does God exist?
2. If God does exist, has he any concern for man's future?
3. If so, what is his particular plan for mankind?

"Ultimo-11 tried to cope. Crammed with all the data of recorded history, it labored hard to produce the right answer. But the effort proved too much for it. All it could gasp was 'Abracadabra... Mandragora... Abra... Gotha... Dada... Ka-ka...' Then it suffered a breakdown.

"Professor Yah patiently repaired its feedback system. Then he programmed his question in a different form:

1. If God does not exist, who made the universe?
2. If God has no concern for man, what should man do about his future?
3. If God has no plan for man, what should man do about God?

69

"Ultimo-11 tried again, scanning its trillions of facts with the speed of light. Then, all at once, with a sudden jingle of alarms and warning bells, it flipped out a small coded card from its innards: 'The information you request is verboten...You need clearance from the Chief...'

"Professor Yah nodded and pushed a red emergency button. The computer shuddered and collapsed. Then the office door marked 'Private' sprung open and God stepped into the laboratory. Professor Yah blinked in surprise. Wearing a long white coat and a long white beard, God seemed an exact replica of Professor Yah, a few inches taller perhaps.

"For a silent moment God glared at Professor Yah. His expression seemed to say: 'You've collected trillions of trivial facts, but lost my Ten Essential Truths!' Then he seized the professor by the collar, marched him back into the private office, and slammed the door behind them. Since then, no one has seen either of them. No one has dared to open the door. And no one has been able to fix the damned computer!"

*   *   *

Malunkyaputta knew he was testing the patience of the Flower Children. But the more he preached, the more his parables multiplied. Like more than one wordy missionary he may have picked up the Mandelbrot Virus, an affliction which led to multiplication, replication, and limitless meandering.

"Let me try one more parable," he said. "By way of a warning... *A Child of the Future.*"

"A team of geneticists wanted to produce a creature who could survive and flourish under the worst conditions. Following a doomsday formula, they synthesized a genetic compound to fertilize a human ovum. They nourished the fetus in an artificial womb. In due time, they delivered the child of the future. Programmed to survive any kind of pollution, the prodigy had superior lungs; he could inhale carbon monoxide, sarin, mustard gas, and other noxious vapors. He had a superior stomach: he could eat arsenic, cyanide, nitric acid or lye without suffering side effects. His skin was impervious to radiation of any kind.

"As a survivor, the creature was successful. But on the other hand, he had the head of a huge blind mole. Instead of hands and feet, he had the claws of a rat. His skin was crocodile skin. He had

70

the nervous system of a rattlesnake. He could not walk, only crawl. He could not talk, only hiss or rattle, and strike."

And Malunkyaputta asked, "Is this your choice for our child of the future?"

Apologizing for his digressions, he pleaded his poet's license. He recited his *Poet's Credo 1*, then closed his sermon.

"Let each of us improve himself as best he can," he said. "Let each one teach himself. Let each of us improve himself and improve the Earth as best he can. Let each of us do something, if only to pull a weed or plant a seed. Compose a new poem or sing a new song!"

For an example, he recited his shortest rhyme:

Noon Song

Noon so clear
     night so long,
Shall I not dare
     invent a song?
Time so little
     change so near,
Words so brittle,
     who will hear?
Let him who can
     turn air to song:
Breath in man
     lasts not long.

The Flower Children heard him resentfully. They couldn't follow the drift of his preaching. They strummed their guitars and hummed nonsense rhymes:

Ma-lunk-lunk-lunk-
Plink-plank-punk-
Ma-ma. Da-da, Ba-ba, Ka-ka-
Mantra, tantra, karma, boo!

It reminded him of the jeer song he had heard in the ashram in Bombay in a former life.

Glancing toward the embankment above the Charles River, he saw three figures strolling along the promenade, dressed in spring finery: a short dark gentleman escorting a stout lady and following a beautiful young girl with a parasol, apparently their daughter. They looked like a family from Seurat's painting of a Sunday promenade. Passing the Flower Children, they bowed to Malunkyaputta and smiled at him distantly, then turned north toward Longfellow's House.

Malunkyaputta heard faint echoes of their singing:

Pad-mini, chit-rini, Padman-Ananda —
Ma-rah, Ma-rah... Dhiri-Dhira...
Mia-Maya... Mu-dita, Ku-lata...
Mantra, tantra, dharma, karma...

He left Boston with mixed feelings. As a missionary, he had met with hostility, contempt, or ridicule. A deepening mystery lay behind the decline of America. Could he discover an answer to the riddle of the Sphinx?

Chapter VII. The Prophet

(1)

To further his edification, Malunkyaputta decided to make a pilgrimage to Washington City. He wanted to witness the bicentennial celebration of Independence on July 4, 1976. He craved to peer into the future. Afflicted with an intense, almost preternatural, curiosity, he wanted to know the shape of things to come. "Whither, America?" he wanted to cry out. "Whither, O visionary people? Whither, unhappy people of America?"

He invented strophes to express his bewilderment:

All men's haven once, the New World's spring of hope:
What spreading haze beclouds your bright horizon?

Whose map or compass will show us the way and tell
where we are this moment and whither bound?

Great things were designed to guide us toward the stars;
yet evils are accomplished in secret every hour...

Whom can we trust to make the right decision?
Whom can we choose to change our direction?

Our banks of computers mislead us;
our masterless agents deceive us...

Our computers have warned us time and again:
"We cannot make the proper decision
without the right information.

The logic we use ends in paradox.
The information we need is not available.

And without the proper information
we cannot make the right decision..."

He composed grim variations on the multiplication table:

The multiplication of facts does not promote understanding.
The multiplication of schools does not promote edification.

The multiplication of judges does not promote justice.
The multiplication of jails does not reduce crime.

The multiplication of asylums does not cure the mad.
The multiplication of people does not improve a country...

He saw multitudes of consumers everywhere, devouring the earth:

"Look behind the walls of any city and behold: Master Death the Insatiable Consumer, with his universal credit card buying up all the perishable goods of the earth, in bags, bins, bottles, barrels, urns and stainless coffins.

"See Father Death and his Unholy Family, sitting in the parlor watching the show, watching the world in a little box, with blind televisionary eyes; forever at home, everywhere, the whole family always together — Papa Todt, Mama Maggot, Brother Grub, Sister Worm — all members of one another, watching and breeding, breeding their ever-multiplying children, our ubiquitous deathlings.

"See Death our Prodigious Pickpocket slyly removing your packet of sense, your invisible purse of rage, reason, passion or compassion; unraveling your manhood; subtracting your eyes, ears, tongue, hair, skin, hands and feet; extracting your heart and the wisdom teeth in your naked skull...

"Listen to the ever-pealing deathbells of your day. Wake up and open your eyes. Can you trap the consuming artist before he catches you? Can you trap the worm of the world in your bag of psalms?"

(2)

Using his old pass, he boarded the train at Penn Station. He carried a knapsack which held his worldly and unworldly goods. A bundle of papers, drafts of new fables and sermons, his rice bowl, a packet of raisins, carrots, a chocolate bar, a few leaves from the Tree of

74

Yggdrasill. When the train halted at a station in Philadelphia, he stepped off on an impulse to visit the historic City of Brotherly Love. He rambled along the waterfront where young Franklin had once sold his Almanac. He looked up the boarding house on Chestnut Street where Jefferson had drafted the Declaration of Independence. He visited Carpenters' Hall where the delegates from the thirteen colonies had once debated the rights of man and the future of America. He roamed about till nightfall, then boarded another train for Washington City.

By the time he reached Union Station, it was past midnight. The capital was pitch black; it seemed deserted; a summer thunderstorm was brewing; and Malunkyaputta didn't know where he might find shelter for the night. He started up a long slope that led through a park toward the great dome of Congress. Before he reached the top of the hill, three muggers jumped on him from the bushes. They were shaggy young fellows who seemed to enjoy their sport. They grabbed his knapsack, searched it, then demanded money. "I haven't any," said Malunkyaputta. They threw the knapsack in his face, knocked him down and ran away.

The thunderstorm broke in a cloudburst and Malunkyaputta was thoroughly drenched. He made his way out of the park toward a lamp post on a street corner at the top of the hill. He didn't know which way to turn.

"Are you lost?" a deep voice asked him out of the darkness.

"I think so," said Malunkyaputta.

A tall black man was standing by his elbow.

"Do you believe in God?" asked the stranger.

"I think so," said Malunkyaputta. "Why not?"

"Do you believe in the Devil?"

"Sometimes. Why not?"

His answer seemed acceptable.

"Follow me!" cried the black Moses. He led Malunkyaputta in the blinding rainstorm through a maze of alleys behind the Library of Congress until they reached an old Victorian boarding house. The black man knocked on the door, which opened to him. The place was a hostel for the homeless, run by Quaker volunteers, in memory of William Penn. Without asking any questions, the good Quakers furnished Malunkyaputta with a bed in the basement.

Waking near noon the next day, he soon discovered the grandeur of the capital. Immensely rich and powerful, the planned city was full of monumental buildings with many-columned marble porches in the style of Greek and Roman temples.   Washington City was grander than Athens or Rome; grander than Jerusalem; grander than Memphis, Thebes, or Babylon. Ringed with green parks and marble statuary, the streets and terraces were filled with multitudes of strollers. Nearly all the people were black. They were the descendants of slaves who had been sold to white planters by black tribal chiefs in Africa two centuries earlier. And they had multiplied. Millions of blacks had moved from plantations in the South to cities in the North — New York, Chicago, Detroit. They had struggled to attain equality. But despite their political emancipation, they remained a caste of pariahs, feared and despised by the whites.

Independence Day on July 4, 1976 was celebrated throughout the land (as John Adams had urged in 1776) with flags, banners, parades with floats and marching bands, and many speeches.   Surrounded by a multitude, Malunkyaputta sat on the steps of the Lincoln Memorial and listened to the orators. The colossal figure of the Great Emancipator was brooding over the crowd. His voice seemed to be speaking through his marble lips, as he spoke at Gettysburg in midst of the Civil War, a war in which a million white men from the North killed a million white men from the South, to free the black slave.

Dedicating the National Cemetery, Lincoln spoke for "a new nation, conceived in liberty, and dedicated to the proposition that all men are created equal…" But in a larger sense, he said, we cannot dedicate this ground. "The brave men, living and dead, who struggled here, have consecrated it far above our poor power to add or detract.

"The world will little note nor long remember what we say here, but it can never forget what they did here.

"It is for us, the living, rather, to be dedicated here to the unfinished work… that these dead shall not have died in vain; that this nation shall have a new birth of freedom; and that government of the people, by the people, for the people, shall not perish from the earth…"

*   *   *

Malunkyaputta heard another speaker at the Lincoln Memorial. A tall thin man with a resonant voice, it was the black Moses who had rescued him in the thunderstorm the night before and led him to the Quaker shelter.

"Come closer, brothers! Follow me! Get the good news," the prophet was summoning his congregation. "It's time for a new birth of freedom, a new Judgment Day, a Grand Awakening! I tell you the truth, and my truth shall set you free—"

A band of strollers joined him, strumming guitars and singing like minstrels:

> We got no fear of Judgment Day,
> Our bones are gonna dance and play —
> Sing Hallelujah!

The black preacher launched his sermon:

" 'All men created equal'? Some more, some less, I'd say. We are stronger and faster than many. Slower than some. Our brains may be smaller. We may have been left behind in the race for an ice age or two. So what? — Great lies have been told against us. White men would keep us in bondage with fables; lock us in jails without bars; shackle our hands and feet with invisible chains! Shall we remain enslaved by white men's lies?

"Hear me, brothers, and learn the truth:

"We come from a mighty people. We are in fact the first fathers of all mankind! Adam and Eve were blacks in the Garden of Eden in Africa. We founded Egypt, and the earliest pharaohs were black. We built the pyramids, we built the Tower of Babel, too. We invented religion, art and science, with singing and dancing and everything good. Moses was a black man. So were the first Hebrews, before they turned into Jews! (Mother Jehovah herself was black in the beginning!)"

Strumming their guitars, the strollers sang:

> We got new shoes to cover our feet!
> We got new skins to cover our bones —
> Sing Hallelujah!

77

The preacher went on with increasing fervor:

"The world will remember what we say here, brothers, as we remember what Ezekiel said when he saw the Valley of Bones in his dream of levitation:

Shall these dry bones that crumble in the darkness,
A barren heap, so marred and charred and broken,
Old shards of faith that hold no living waters,
Reclothe themselves in flesh when I have spoken?
And feel a fresh wind blowing through the breastbone,
The heart like wild wings beating in its hollows?

Then rise, pale bones, and wrap yourselves in sinew:
The spell that bound you to the pit is broken.
Find living eyes and heart and hope within you:
Roll out into the sun — the grave is open.
Now celebrate the breath that stirs within you,
O twice-burned bones twice-born — the word is spoken!"

The strollers sang:

O bones twice burned
and bones twice-born:
Sing Hallelujah!

The black prophet cried out: " 'A new birth of freedom'? Why not? What's been the good of dying white man's science? Or the good of his history? His science but magnified his power to enslave us. His history: a long chronicle of crimes. His books are filled with lies or base conjectures! — Our brains may be smaller, but we can breed faster. That's the secret weapon. And that's our mission: We'll outbreed our masters and bury them! — O blessed are we, brothers, for we shall inherit the works!"

The strollers sang in response:

We shall inherit the works,
We'll burn the books and break the chains —
We blacks will be masters; the whites, our slaves —
Sing Hallelujah!

A fire with invisible flames was consuming a city fairer than Athens or Rome. The marble halls and temples were toppling, turned into ruins by all-devouring time, as if by an earthquake and tidal wave, a meteor, a hydrogen bomb. The site of the once great city a burning dump with a roiling crater. Multitudes of scavengers were swarming over Necropolis, feeding the crater with trash and treasure. They were burning five million books from the Library of Congress, including the works of Plato, Aristotle, Lucretius; Virgil, Dante, Shakespeare; Newton, Goethe, Galileo. (They were true believers burning the dead white fathers as if burning the Library of Alexandria.) They were burning documents from the Archives: the Declaration, the Constitution, the Bill of Rights; the letters of Franklin, Jefferson, Washington; old treaties, records, maps and manifestoes. A thousand portraits from the National Gallery. The bones of ten thousand Indian skeletons from the Smithsonian. Bundles of greenbacks from the Treasury. A million patents from the Patent Office. Tons of drugs, tapes, films, and a mountain of dishes from gourmet restaurants. Thousands of TV sets, shoes, uniforms; leather bags, eye glasses, microscopes; guns, model planes, rockets; condoms and embryos...

*   *   *

At the foot of the crater, apart from the multitude of shadows, Malunkyaputta thought he could see three scavengers, his old familiars, sorting the waste and commenting on their findings. He thought he recognized his old friends in the guise of a stern Dump-master, a stout Rag-picker, and a beauteous Treasure-finder. They seemed to him as real as anyone he ever knew; as real or as transient and insubstantial. Though they were sorting fast, they could hardly keep up with the torrents of change.

He thought he could hear their voices:

" — The turning wheel converts the real into illusion."
" — So the poor become rich with the goods of the world.
     And the rich become poor, despite their treasures..."
" — Yet out of the ashes may grow a new garden.
     Out of the ruins may rise a new temple..."
" — O Breaker of Worlds: Design a new thing!
     Breeder of Death: Make a thing that may sing —"

Behind the burning dumps, he thought he could hear the chant of a choir, mourning the holocaust:

> Behold our lost shepherd
> shaking his staff against
> the burning tree of life
> and his desperate children
> in a cloud of smoke.

> Behold our dying father, blind with grief,
> stumbling from a molten garden,
> driving the shadows before him
> down the long slope of the evening
> toward the brink of the night.

> Behold him drowning in a blood-dark sea,
> melding into the gathering haze,
> and see him fading behind the smoke,
> an ever-thickening veil of ashes...

Chapter VIII. The Messiah

After a long season of trials and errors, nearly the age of forty, Malunkyaputta left the East Coast and set up his camp on Mount Palomar in California. A high point in a majestic wilderness, Mount Palomar was crowned by a modern astronomical observatory. It had broad stone steps in front of it, a parapet around it and, below it, a long terrace with a swimming pool.

On a Sunday in Eastertide, Malunkyaputta descended the broad steps, intending to deliver a special message to his followers and fellow pilgrims. He wanted to give them a revelation that would set them free from bondage. "Awaken, beloved people," he wanted to say. "Awaken from your never-ending dream of lust and desire and suffering. Escape from the old wheel of birth and death. Listen to the truth that will set you free…"

Barefooted, half-wrapped in a worn dhoti, he made a meagre figure, despite his messianic aims, and the crowd on the terrace ignored his vocalizing. He surveyed the jubilant assembly and recognized some of his earlier followers: converts from the Rockefeller Center, marchers from the Bowery, Flower Children from Boston and Washington. He saw many strangers too, weaving and bobbing in a hurly-burly of nude merrymakers.

Male and female, a mixed company of nymphs and satyrs, they were celebrating their New Age freedom with total abandon. They were playing the games prescribed in the Kama Sutra. Some masturbated each other; licked and swallowed, bit and chewed each other. Some copulated in a goatish frenzy. They searched each other's bodies for new sex-holes. They rubbed their skins together, to stimulate or simulate fresh orgasms.

Rubbing their skins together was their chief source of pleasure. The oldest skin game on earth, it was pursued by every creature, from fleas to elephants, from rats to baboons, from Jukes to Kallikaks. Despite an overcrowded earth, the post-Neanderthals were bent on breeding and multiplying.

Malunkyaputta observed a variety of perversions. Sodomy, coprophilia, flagellation. Some were whipping the buttocks, punishing or torturing their mates; some craved to be hurt and humiliated; some wanted to suffer the sharpest pains, in an effort to satisfy their fantasies. It was a hidden part of their fertility rites.

Malunkyaputta looked for a way to halt the bestial carnival. But no one paid any attention to him.

Then a band of newcomers joined the party.

Shaggy young men carrying a huge tent, they seemed to spring from the wilderness below Mount Palomar. They formed a circle around the swimming pool, raised the tent, and began ceremony. Pretending to be pregnant, they imitated women in labor. They moaned and groaned. They danced and acted out a painful delivery. A childbearing rite, the *couvade* was an old custom which may have derived from the dream-time of tribes in Australia, Papua, New Guinea, Java, Bali, Fiji, Lesotho, Alabama, Manhattan or other exotic places.

Malunkyaputta observed the performers: The young men were hopping in and out of the tent screaming and howling, pretending to be women in labor. They were imitating their birth pangs.   Some were wailing in a piercing falsetto like newborn infants.   Some were shaking wooden rattles or bells. Others were beating their chests as if beating a drum. A few were laughing uproariously.

Malunkyaputta raised his voice in an effort to stop them. But he could not be heard under the young men's noise-making. Was he denouncing their circus and predicting Judgment Day in his exalted doomsday style? "Behold our ignorant brothers building their monstrous birth-stools! Behold them girding their loins for the bloody travail! Behold them grinding their teeth and bearing down to deliver their progeny. Behold death's fathers in their nursery of deathlings! Behold ten thousand new children, condemned to die of hunger..."

He heard children's voices crying from a distance:

> "Mouths forever moving,
> our hunger never ceases.
> Mouths forever searching,
> our hunger never eases..."

Malunkyaputta came down the stone steps and moved closer to the dancers. "Behold our demented brothers, bewildered by lust, all rushing deathward…"

A dancer shouted, "Cut out his tongue!"

Malunkyaputta stepped toward the tent and seized its main frame as if to tear it down. "You breathe the air of decay and never know it! You dance in the wake of death and never know it…" He shook the tent.

The dancers turned on Malunkyaputta. "Stone him!" they shouted. "Stone the false prophet!"

They pinioned his arms. They hustled him up the stairs. They dragged him to the top of the Observatory. They wanted to fling him into the canyon below.

To be stoned by his disciples; this was the fate of more than one prophet. Was this the destined end of Malunkyaputta? But he was allergic to martyrdom. So he shook them off. "Will you never learn a new thing?" he cried. "Did Malunkyaputta teach you nothing? Slaves of your father's fables, you'd treat Malunkyaputta the way you treated your best teachers: Socrates, Jesus, Gandhi, Vivekananda… I gave you my wealth, I gave you whatever I had of wisdom. You'd stone me on Mount Palomar! Perfidious cretins. Ungrateful clowns!"

Had he been stoned on Mount Palomar, he might have been beatified and his name would be canonized by the Latter-Day Sons of Saint Malunkyaputta. But few prophets could choose the right day for dying; few martyrs were lucky enough to pick the best time for their exit. Like aging actors they tended to wear out their welcome with too many return engagements. Malunkyaputta shook off his attackers, then fixed them with his glittering eyes. He was filled with the righteous rage of Zarathustra, both as the old Persian prophet and as his avatar in Basle.

"Day and night you devour the fruits of the Earth like a plague of locusts," he cried. "Day and night, you multiply like rats or lemmings. Day and night, you breed new legions for Hunger and Famine. You devour your children like cannibals. Day and night, you repeat your fathers' blunders. You'd turn the whole Earth into a dump of breeders…"

He stepped toward the parapet that overlooked the great valley. "I despise the odious race. I hate the whole tribe. I reject the

Breeders — Breeders, defective, insatiable, incorrigible!" He climbed the parapet and half turned toward the angry crowd which pressed closer to him. "I came to teach the Untouchable. I leave to curse the Unteachable!"

He turned from them, and some ran toward him in a rage, determined to catch and kill their insufferable prophet. Eluding his pursuers, he leaped from the parapet and fled into the wilderness.

* * *

At the far end of the terrace, his three old friends had re-appeared as a modest TV crew to film his performance. Padman was director; Precious Lady Stepmother acted as reporter; Mia operated the camera. It was an old-fashioned camera with a crank, a model which had been used by Pathe News before World War One.

They criticized his performance.

"A preposterous actor," said Precious Lady Stepmother.

"He's blind to the obvious. As always," said Padman.

"He's caught in his web of delusions," said Mia.

"He suffers from a False Messiah complex," said Precious Lady Stepmother.

"It's the millennial season again," Padman observed. "The woods are crawling with messiahs. And more than one is begging to be stoned..."

"Will our poor friend ever be edified?" asked Mia. "Will he learn the truth from our experiment?"

Part Three

Progress Report

Said the Man of False Views to a Man of Few Words:
"Change is upon us. The times are evolutionary.
Our future must not be bound by our past!"

Said the Man of Few Words to the Man of False Views:
"Progress is regressive. The times are devolutionary.
Change: an illusion. The future will mirror the past..."

Chapter IX. The Hermit

After his escape from Mount Palomar, Malunkyaputta made his way through the wilderness, tramping northward along the rugged Pacific coast for nearly 1000 miles. For weeks he hiked along Highway #1, passing Big Sur, Point Lobos, Monterey, Santa Cruz. Near Mendocino he turned inland and eastward until at last he reached Mount Shasta. An extinct volcano capped with snow, set in a wild and solitary country, in a ring of volcanoes, Mount Shasta became his home. On a lower slope of the mountain, he built a log cabin for his hermitage.

Malunkyaputta cultivated a kitchen garden and raised crops of vegetables, chiefly corn, potatoes, and beans. He brooded over the past and cultivated his grievances. He reviewed his efforts to help the people, their failure to grasp his message, their rejection of his gospel of Science. He repeated his mantra with minor variations: "I despise mankind. I hate the hypocritical breeders who infest the Earth. I hate and fear the murderous tribe. I'd like to secede from the human race!" He had good reasons to fear his fellowmen.

He thought of composing a short true history of mankind in which he could epitomize the evolution of human stupidity. But what could he report that wasn't common knowledge? And whom could he entertain with the truth, except himself? Everyone knew too much and not enough. They blundered blindly in the rut of their deluded fathers.

What more could he tell them?

*　*　*

Everyone knew the oldest story. Life began in the sea about four billion years ago. The single-celled bacteria multiplied. They formed fish-and-plant life about 400 million years ago. They crawled out of the sea in a company of worms and slugs and snails, and learned to breathe air. They evolved into scaly reptiles, along with scorpions, toads, and the cockroach, about fifty million years ago. The new crawlers colonized the coastland and floated with the drifting continents. They learned to lay eggs for their brood. They became warm-blooded mammals. They grew hair and feathers.

The creature who turned into Early Man about three million years ago developed grasping hands and grasping eyes and grasping brains. Resembling a wild but increasingly crafty and aggressive monkey, he became a beast of prey. He stalked the mammoth and the mastodon. During a million years of the intermittent Ice Ages, he survived in caves. He learned to make fire. He learned to manipulate sounds to make speech. He invented fables of demons or gods, and a life after death.

After the glaciers melted, he emerged from the cave and lived in the greening savannahs and bushlands. The first modern man appeared 40,000 years ago; the most recent Ice Age ended 10,000 years ago. This marked the beginning of civilization. Man learned to plant crops. Passing from the hunter and gatherer stage, he learned to tame half-wild animals: the ox, the boar, the horse, while he himself remained a beast of prey. He learned to wage war. He learned to breed faster than rats or lemmings. He learned to build great towns and cities. He raised Stonehenge; the Pyramids; the Parthenon. Survivor of the Ice Ages, modern man was the inheritor of Egypt, Greece and Rome. He was the heir of Buddha, Confucius, Plato; Socrates, Jesus, Aristotle; Newton, Darwin, Edison, Einstein.

And how did post-modern man spend his time?

Despite his grand legacy and good luck in the lottery of life, he remained a garrulous and quarrelsome cousin of the chimpanzees. Though his recent ancestors had built the Cathedral of Notre Dame, the most advanced people in Europe had built Auschwitz and Buchenwald. His current leaders, the politicians, generals, global traders and arms dealers to whom he gave power, prestige, wealth, the prizes of democracy, were promoting old fables and superstitions, exploiting his greed and fears, dividing and ruling the people. Rather than the survival of the fittest, they were promoting the survival of the fiercest or greediest. As always.

How did he spend his three score years and ten? Anyone could compose Adam's resume:

"Of my three score years and ten, I spent twenty years in bed, asleep, farting or fucking. Twenty years working, playing, or fighting. Ten years praying and preying. Seven years eating and drinking. Three years shitting and pissing. A month in meditating the meaning of it all. A week in the hospital, trying to die well and dying ill…"

*   *   *

Malunkyaputta converses with his imaginary visitors. Aristophanes said: "Brek-kek-kek! …" Confucius said: "Rectify your Speech." Socrates said: "Know your self."

"But we're past all that!" Malunkyaputta said.

Moses said: "No!" Zarathustra said: "Ho!" Wittgenstein said: "Ha!"

"But we're past all that!" Malunkyaputta said. "We now say simply: Ka-ka-ka!"

*   *   *

In spite of his misanthropic reflections, he felt that something more was at work behind the scenes. Something important was still eluding him.

*   *   *

He added a fable to his journal: *"A Monkey on Mount Palomar…"*

"Late one night, when a wildfire threatened to burn down the coast, a monkey escaped from the zoo in San Diego. Making his way through the smoking brush, he reached the observatory on Mount Palomar. He climbed up into the tower and searched the place, but found no sign of life. The tower was dark and abandoned. The astronomers had left the Earth in a rocket ship; they were lost or exploring the outermost edge of space.

"The monkey began to inspect the abandoned station. Wrapping himself in a lab coat, he lit a torch and tested some of the apparatus. When he pressed certain keys in a console of computers, laser beams of light appeared overhead. The dome of the observatory slid open and a giant telescope began to rotate slowly, its inner lens or eye turning into the curving disk of Hubble's Mirror. Imposed on it was a star map of the universe. A receding cluster of lights, the cosmic cloud of galaxies was drifting outward in slow motion, seemingly finite yet infinite, without beginning or end.

"The monkey peered into the telescope. He stared at the star map. He stared at his own hairy image in Hubble's Mirror. The images were clear yet seemed mystifying. Searching further, he opened a locker at the foot of the telescope and consulted a manual. An atlas of equations, it contained a review of the laws of physics, and an index of paradoxes and final solutions and a summary of all the Grand Unified & Partial Theories of the Universe. The curious monkey pored over the equations. He studied them with increasing dissatisfaction. Observing the unresolved anomalies, he shook his head.

"Then he discovered a report on the history of Hubble's Mirror. The huge disk had been designed and built by the best optical engineers at an astronomical cost. But in grinding the lens, they had miscalculated the curvature by a billionth of an inch. This infinitesimal error, it seems, had affected both the star map and the fate of the missing astronauts. Veering from their trajectory in outer space, they had been sucked in by a black hole and vanished without a trace.

" 'Preposterous men!' our monkey cried out in a fit of fury. 'So proud and demented! Your mirror is flawed, your star map is false! You aim to be godlike, but remain a prey to your delusions!'

"In a fit of rage the monkey broke the computer's console and smashed Hubble's Mirror. With his flaming torch he set fire to the Observatory. He laughed and ran from Mount Palomar back into the wilderness!"

Malunkyaputta imitated the monkey's malicious laughter. Then asked:

"What does this mean? It means that our monkey wants to reject the works of science. It means that if you act like monkeys, my savage friends, you may become a band of deaf monkeys howling in the wilderness!"

*   *   *

He thought he heard the voices of his old friends, conversing in what seemed to be the ruins of a temple in Cambodia.

"He barely escaped with his life," said Padman-Ananda. "Another turn of the Wheel..."

"I saved him from death by drowning," said Our Precious Lady Stepmother.

"I saved him from boredom," said Mia.

"He fears his former disciples," said Padman. "He hates his neighbors as he hates himself. He despises his fellows... Will he learn to read the future?"

"He pursues a false trail," said Our Precious Lady Stepmother. "How can he be edified?"

"Will he recognize his condition?" asked Mia. "Can he bear the truth?"

Chapter X. The Clown

To entertain himself in his solitary cabin, Malunkyaputta improvised bawdy songs from time to time. These reflected his contempt for his ever-multiplying fellowmen. He sang his scurrilous rhymes to himself in a harsh voice, punctuated by fits of scornful laughter. Indulging in poetic license, he felt free to mock whatever he pleased, often pushing his efforts beyond the limits of common sense or decorum. In due time, he collected one hundred scats in a set which he called *Malunkyaputta's Prolegomena to Breaking Wind*. At intervals, warmed by his favorite liqueurs, he'd sing his scats from midnight to dawn.

One night, while a snow storm was brewing on Mount Shasta, he conjured up his three old friends from the Ganges to join his party and share his songs. Ten years had passed since their last meeting on Mount Palomar, though time seemed to have no effect on them. They gathered in various parts of the cabin, which was hazy with smoke from a wood fire. He filled their glasses from his stock of cointreau, kummel, and benedictine. Our Precious Lady Stepmother was wearing a huge flowery red robe like a gypsy queen; she was telling false fortunes with a pack of Tarot cards which fluttered in her hands like a necklace of rubies or sparks from the stove. Professor Padman, who looked like a seedy schoolmaster, was playing chess with a chimpanzee who somehow resembled Padman himself and who managed to Checkmate his partner. Mia was gliding about the dim room slowly, as if imitating Salome in her Dance of the Seven Veils. This went on for a few moments, till Malunkyaputta adjusted his eyes to his visitors.

He then bowed to them and sang in a solo, *An Introduction*:

> Behold, Preposterous Me,
> And behold Preposterous You!
> A fact like anyone else,
> A simple fact, a sample fact,
> Yet remarkable as any fact!

A ghost among ghosts in a dance of dreams,
A knot of worms in a box of bones:
The riddle of the universe —
Preposterous Me and Preposterous You!
(How clever of us to discover this too!)

He refilled their glasses and his friends now sang to him in a cheerful trio *An Invitation*:

Come join the dance,
the dance of the May-flies.
Join, conjoin! oh, what a surprise!
For some, the game of games.
For some, a fateful exercise.
For all, a fatal enterprise!
May-flies deflowering the buds of spring,
all join the dance of the birds and the bees.
Join, they sing, come join! Share our surprise!

Malunkyaputta sang in solo *The Question*:

Am I clever? Am I wise?
Do I sniff a fresh surprise?
Breaking wind with cautious art,
Do I crap or merely fart?

His friends joined in a chorus, improvising a madrigal and, with Malunkyaputta keeping time like a choirmaster, sang *From Genesis to Revelations*:

From the Pyramids to the Pyranees,
Girls have learned to spread their knees.
From Eden to Kalamazoo
They teach the boys to hump and screw.

Oh, they fucked in the Garden,
They fuck at home;
They fucked in Egypt,
They fuck in Rome!

Yes, it's fuck, fuck, fuck!
It's always fuck or fight.
They fuck fast in the daylight
But faster in the night!

If you fear you haven't juice enough
to electrify Diana,
Fuck Moses, Holy Mary,
Or Ma and Pa Jehovah!

Then Malunkyaputta delivered a solo again, impersonating a
street preacher, while strumming an imaginary guitar:

All my life I was a secret sinner, yea, all my life!
A boy on the farm I played in the barn,
I played with myself and spilled my seed,
Oh yes, like Onan, I spilled my seed in the hay!
I frolicked in the meadow with my father's flock,
I gamboled with the sheep and the goats,
I fornicated day and night, like the gay folk in Gomorrah. —
O Lord, how I have sinned, how I have sinned!

I tumbled with whores, from Little Rock to Babylon.
I tumbled with Maggie on Market Street;
I tumbled with Bella, Carmen, Donna by the Golden Gate;
I tumbled with my neighbors' wives in rented rooms;
I tumbled with many without paying a penny;
Night or day, I tumbled whenever I could.
O Lord, how I have sinned, how I have sinned!

When I preached the gospel in Babylon,
I taught the most rousing lessons to each and all.
I taught them in Sunday School, I taught them in the choir;
I never hid my light under a bush;
I fornicated wherever I could.
I lusted for little girls and lusted for boys as well.
I mounted their mothers and pleasured their grandmothers.
O Lord, how I have sinned, how I have sinned!

I played with my flock like the gay folk in Gomorrah.
I stole the widow's mite and preached like an angel.
I practiced prevarications of every kind —
Simony, sodomy, adultery, hypocrisy!
Punish me, Lord, do not spare the rod:
I've been unworthy of my mission:
My abominations are without name or number —
O Lord, how I have sinned, how I have sinned!

His friends laughed at his lusty impersonation and responded with a jubilant chorus, *Biblical Blues*, which sounded like an old-fashioned spiritual:

God's First Farts are recorded in Genesis,
    His Last Farts in Revelations.

His First Farts are called the Chosen;
    His Last Farts are the Rejected.

His First Farts claim they're elected,
    His Last Farts claim they're selected.

But God can fart in any way he chooses!
    Sing Hallelujah!

No one can call the least of his farts
    Chosen, Rejected, Elected or Selected.

God farts and farts at random for ever
    Breaking wind in gales and whirlwinds,

Filling the air with millions of moons,
    Turning the wheel for billions of galaxies,

Worlds within worlds, forever and a day!
    Sing Hallelujah!

Outside, a great blizzard was raging as if trying to tear apart the huge black wilderness. Inside the warm cabin, while his imaginary friends were singing his bawdy blues, Malunkyaputta danced around the smoky room. Sometimes, his friends wove variations on his lines, converting his rude rhymes into villanelles. Sometimes, he joined in a chorus with them, chanting in a rumbling sing-song which resembled Sanskrit:

"Padmini, Chitrini, Shankhini...
  Mudita, Kulata, Kamagarvita.
  Divyadivya, Divyadivya...
  Tantra, Mantra, Dharma, Karma..."

He was imitating a free spirit dancing in cosmic space-time, beyond all human limitations. He was dancing with beauteous Mia. He was dancing with Precious Lady Stepmother.

"*Who* are you now, Malunkyaputta?" asked Precious Lady Stepmother with a sly and watchful smile. "Quibbler? Quester? Faucet-inventor— ?"

"No one. Anyone!" cried Malunkyaputta. "Call me whatever you like—"

Padman chimed in: "Teacher? Preacher? Pornographer? Clown— ?"

"I played many parts!" cried Malunkyaputta. "I searched for my self. I led many lives — "

"Poet or philosopher?" asked Mia.

"Born again, lost again, I don't know what I am," said Malunkyaputta.

He joined hands with his friends to form a circle and they whirled around the room deliriously until they became a transient blue in the turning wheel of time. Then his friends faded away. And Malunkyaputta found himself alone again.

* * *

Sipping another glass of kummel, he thought he heard his friends whispering from a great distance.

"Well, Malunkyaputta, what have you learned? With all your freedom to pursue your way; to sing and dance and explore a world of ten thousand revelations: what have you accomplished? What have you discovered that no one knew before?"

Malunkyaputta echoed their whispers. He resolved to change his bad habits and learn something new about himself and the world. There was something mysterious at work behind the scene, a secret he had yet to discover.

He rambled in this vein for awhile, talking to himself before falling asleep:

"Alas, my friend, you played the clown again... Chronic self-deluder, blunderer: How much longer will you reel after shadows or people the night with guests of your fantasy? What crimes men commit in the name of freedom. What sad lessons we learn in the school for joy! O the sorrow of the bawdy, the pangs of pleasure, the blunder of dying unedified.... Bless Aristotle, bless Aristophanes, bless Rosencrantz and Wittgenstein, bless Kant of Konigsberg with his ding and his dong! O the comfort of Illusion, the joys of the Absurd. The blessing of Ignorance. The bliss of Oblivion...."

Chapter XI. The Journal-Keeper

(1)

Malunkyaputta kept a journal for company the way other men kept a dog, a wolf cub, or a mistress. He shared with it his secrets. The Journal became his defense against boredom and despair; loss of memory, amnesia, oblivion; it was his shelter from the eroding wheel of time and the irreversible seasons. So his days on Mount Shasta unraveled in a procession of stormy springs and snow-bound winters, the months turned into years, the years into decades, and his Journal grew in volume, filling thousands of pages. Instead of talking to himself in an old man's quavering voice, Malunkyaputta talked to himself on paper. An inexpensive pleasure which he pursued for more than twenty years.

Sitting by his kitchen table in the rude log cabin, he wrote and wrote in a looseleaf binder night after night reporting his conversations with himself. He reported his opinions about everything; his past blunders and vanities; his recurrent doubts and speculations. He enlivened his hermit's log with jingles, riddles, dreams and fables.

The Journal would reveal his true history, he believed. By reporting the odd facts and fantastic truths of his experience he would come to know himself. His chronicle would contain all the clues he needed for capturing his real identity. It was his last best method for attaining self-edification. It should lead to the Venerable Malunkyaputta, a confounded old quibbler and quester, to Total and Final Enlightenment!

After all, wasn't this his lifelong goal? The Journal was perhaps, his final experiment in discovering the answers to his first and last questions: "Who am I? Why am I? What is my meaning?" The Greeks had carved an answer to their secrets on the lintel of their marble temple at Delphi, a seat of their oracles: *"Know Your Self."* Socrates had studied himself as closely as he did his elusive fellows in Athens. "The unexamined life is not worth living," said Socrates. Yet sometimes Malunkyaputta himself would wonder: "Is a much-examined life more worth living?"

In his wayward youth he had searched for edification by studying the best philosophers. They did not make him wiser. He had searched for a book with answers to his first and last questions. "I looked for it in the world's great libraries. What I found did not satisfy me. A medley of facts and fantasy, the books raised more questions than they answered. I found no single work which satisfied me. Later I told myself: There's no such work. All the books in the libraries are but fragments of fragments or drafts from future works. The book I crave may be in the book of nature. Timely and timeless, that book is coded in the spiraling script of atoms and molecules. If only I had time and wit enough to decipher a single line of it!"

A quester by the garbage-strewn banks of the Ganges, he had once hoped to gain the world's esteem as a poet. Not a minor poet, of whom there were too many; but a universal bard, to outshine the best. He had wanted to compose songs to mirror the heart and soul of mankind; to reflect Everyman's passionate feelings and reveal the real and the transcendental. He had declared his poet's decalog while preaching on Mount Palomar:

"I will celebrate all things under the stars and furnish my suffering neighbors with fresh springs of delight..." Despite his efforts he had been rejected. Why? Because he composed his songs in Sanskrit when all the world spoke only Esperanto? Or, vice-versa, because he wrote in Esperanto when the world knew only Sanskrit? Since then he had learned the language of silence and solitude. He spoke in a language no one understood. As someone had observed: If a lion revealed his secrets in a lion's language, the jackals would not understand him.

The millennium was approaching: It was time to close his Journal.

He had many more things to report, of course, but he was running out of time. Moreover, he now suspected that keeping a Journal as a way of discovering his identity was another delusion. How could he know himself when he was constantly changing? How could any arrangement of words furnish a map or a mirror to reflect his true state of mind? He tried to report his immediate states of awareness. But his awareness was in a perpetual flux. He altered every day, minute by minute. He changed his mental coloration like a frenetic chameleon. He could never predict what his next mood or state of mind might be. The more he examined himself, the less he understood; the more he reported, the less he knew. What might he conclude from this? The self was elusive or illusory. It was a process, not a steady state. An unfolding and ever-changing process, from birth to death. A process to be endured, not comprehended.

After passing three score years and ten, he indulged himself in speculation on his fast-approaching end. Like more than one senescent theologian, he passed from scatological to eschatological ruminations. A man might live a hundred years or a hundred and fifty, yet did anyone ever outwit death? Did anyone reverse his irreversible last performance? No, not even the strongest or cleverest. Our birth certificate was also our death certificate.

Malunkyaputta added a reminder to himself in his *Journal*, addressing himself in the style of Marcus Aurelius:

"All the crowds of young men and women we see in the streets of the world, laughing, singing, shouting, raging, pursuing each other, pursuing their vivid or dismal illusions, all will have left the scene in less than a century. All our contemporaries are transients. Our vast assemblies are, in a sense, a supernatural or ghostly crowd. And the present instant, alive in myself as the writer of these lines and in you as their reader, is a vanishing point. We both are engaged in a ghostly enterprise. All that we boast as our works or revelations, all that we build and launch for the stars, all that we will, scheme, dare and dream, all that we do is perishable. The labor of our hands: a mound of ashes. Our book for the ages: a thing of dust. Our dearest child: a passing creature of perpetual change. All our works, borrowed from usurious Time, all are perishable. Advancing toward us, inexorably, our last invincible friend and enemy: Time in his dust-gray cowl; Time with his legions of scavengers. Time with his slow invisible feet, each step of which weighs a trillion tons, since his step will press us into the everlasting dust and calm our fevers forever."

(2)

Occasionally, he reported fragments of his dreams. The dreams of an old man were brief but vivid, often absurd. Properly interpreted, they might furnish clues to the future. Malunkyaputta believed that dreams were an original language from the prehistoric past, when man was a dreaming, speculative, telepathic animal and shared his dream-language with other animals.

In quest of self-knowledge, he reported his dreams and visions; his dark dreams and his wet dreams; his ancient duel with Krishna in the Ramayana; his amorous encounters with Our Precious Lady Stepmother and Mia. At times his Journal resembled an unraveling phantasmagoria. Was he losing his reason? Was he becoming a demented hermit in the solitary wilderness? Whenever he trimmed his shaggy beard and looked into his shaving mirror — the little round mirror which his stepmother had given him in a former life — he saw an increasingly dark and unfamiliar face.

Malunkyaputta liked the old Chinese poem about a man who had dreamt that he was a butterfly. The old poet Chuang-Tse, a contemporary of Meng-Tse (372-280 B.C.), remained puzzled by his dream.

Waking in his garden one afternoon, Chuang-Tse asked himself: "Am I a man who dreamt that he's a butterfly, or am I a butterfly now dreaming that I am a man?"

In some of his dreams Malunkyaputta met with Our Precious Lady Step-Mother. Nude, white-haired, and very old, she'd improvise a sacred dance before him. At times she also appeared young and wore the enchanting mask of Mia, the love of his youth, still infinitely beautiful and desirable.

He drafted a few lines to report this recurrent dream:

> When I looked on my mother's nakedness,
> I was lost in a cloud of remembrance.
>
> When I looked on my beloved's nakedness,
> I was spellbound and muted.
>
> When I looked on my own nakedness
> below the moon in a sea of stars,
>
> I beheld a world unraveling in mystery,
> unveiling its beauty.
>
> Lost in a cloud of remembrance
> I was spellbound and muted...

At times, his whole life now seemed to him a series of dream-fragments. His quest for edification resembled a private phantasmagoria. His Journal itself was but an ever-expanding Dream Book.

*   *   *

What was the answer? At times he heard Padman-Ananda's sharp voice echoing in his ears: "Buddha gave you the answer a long time ago. He told you the cause and taught you the cure for man's unhappiness and recurrent sorrows. He told you the truth. But you chose not to understand. You chose to question and quibble. You fled from the golden flood of his illumination to pursue your delusive quest of Self-edification. Your self? A mirage, a shadow in a world of shadows! You wasted the master's gift of wisdom for a beggar's bowl of delusions...   And where has it brought you? Pursuing your little self, you have lost your greater self."

Who am I?   Malunkyaputta wondered. He had lived so many lives he no longer knew his boundaries or his true identity.

He found a curious paper in his collection of Buddhist scriptures, a paper which reported his ancient quarrel with Buddha around 500 B.C.   Preserved in Tibet for more than two thousand years, it was a translation of Sutta 63 from the Majjhima-Nikaya and was titled *On Questions Which Tend Not To Edification*. Malunkyaputta read Buddha's sermon with attention, though he recalled the distant occasion in a rather vague transcendental light.   In so far as the scriptures were creditable, Buddha himself furnished proof of Malunkyaputta's historical existence.

"Malunkyaputta, you have not said to me, 'Reverend Sir, I will lead the religious life on condition that The Blessed One elucidate to me either that the world is eternal, or that the world is not eternal, ... or that the saint neither exists nor does not exist after death.'   That being the case, vain man, whom are you so angrily denouncing? ...

"It is as if, Malunkyaputta, a man had been wounded by an arrow thickly smeared with poison, and his friends and companions, his relatives and kinsfolk, were to procure for him a physician or surgeon; and the sick man were to say, 'I will not have this arrow taken out until I have learnt whether the man who wounded me was tall, or short, or of the middle height.' ...

"Or again he were to say, 'I will not have this arrow taken out until I have learnt whether the shaft which wounded me was

101

wound round with the sinews of an ox, or of a buffalo, or of a ruru deer, or of a monkey.' ...

"The religious life, Malunkyaputta, does not depend on the dogma that the world is eternal; nor does the religious life, Malunkyaputta, depend on the dogma that the world is not eternal. Whether the dogma obtain, Malunkyaputta, there still remain birth, old age, death, sorrow, lamentation, misery, grief, and despair, for the extinction of which in the present life I am prescribing.

"Or on the dogma that the world is finite; ... that the soul and the body are identical; ... that the saint exists and does not exist after death; ... These questions I have not elucidated. Because, Malunkyaputta, this profits not, nor has to do with the fundamentals of religion, nor tends to aversion, absence of passion, cessation, quiescence, the supernatural faculties, supreme wisdom, and Nirvana.

"Bear always in mind what it is that I have not explained and what it is that I have explained... And what *have* I explained, Malunkyaputta? Misery have I explained: the origin of misery, the cessation of misery, and the path leading to the cessation of misery have I explained."

(3)

Approaching his 80th birthday, Malunkyaputta prepared for his exit. "How much time have I left?" he asked himself. "All things are on fire, all things are burning..." Buddha had told him in a former life. Indeed, the world was burning with invisible flames and all things were perpetually crumbling. Sometimes he wanted to warm his quibbling bones in the golden light of the Compassionate Buddha, who had sought the truth, after all, despite the obfuscations of his myriad, latter-day, pious and unholy followers. Buddha had taught the way to Nirvana. Yet what was Nirvana? A return to the womb, the womb of the All-Devouring Mother, the black hole of the Cosmos? Or an escape from Chaos into nothingness? A veil for man's secret Death-wish?

"What should I do?" Malunkyaputta asked himself. "Study the fragmentation of Mount Shasta or the erosion of the Himalayas? ... Rejoice in the Now, for it's all I have, and all I may know of the Hereafter? ... How much time have I left?" He was on the verge of becoming permanently muted and invisible. Everyman's story, of course, yet not too pleasing a curtain. To die

102

incomplete, riddled with ignorance; to die, alas, before we are truly edified!

At times, he felt sharp intimations of his imminent end. At times, he felt on the edge of a great awakening. Intermittently, he felt that death itself was another illusion, a change of form in a perpetual dance of forms.

From time to time, he played host to imaginary visitors if and held conversations with the dead.

"You too are mortal, my friend," Socrates told him.

"I don't believe it," said Malunkyaputta.

"All men must die, sooner or later," Aristophanes told him.

"I don't believe it," said Malunkyaputta.

"The longer you live the more certain your end," Aristotle told him.

"I don't believe it," said Malunkyaputta.

Nevertheless, he prepared for his exit.

Malunkyaputta added a page to his Posthumous Psalms.

THE ALMIGHTY MICROCHIP

Who'll invent a new psalm for God,
    Our First Almighty Microchip,
        the microscopic egg
            of an ever-expanding universe?

Who'll compose an ode for the atoms,
    the ever-dancing atoms that flow
        through funnels of chaos toward cosmos,
            the atoms inside your skull?

Who'll discover himself in a mirror,
    the mirror of the galaxies
        that mirrors the mind of God,
            a force that shapes both grasshoppers
            and hummingbirds,
        yet may prove mad to our understanding?

Who'll answer the riddle behind the stars,
    the ever-receding galaxies
        and our ever-deepening Mystery?

103

* * *

He added snapshots of himself to his Journal:

A KING OF DECEMBER

I cross a rain-swollen stream
its white foam bubbling frothily over the rocks.
I walk through drifts of pine branches in the flood.

Stripped of my greenery in the middle of the woods,
my branches barren of leaves;
snow covers my head like a wintry cowl.

Ignorance knots my brow and
presses on me a crown of brambles.
Once king of the May, I've become
a graybeard of December.

Beard is torn by the winds of winter
ruffled by gales of December's laughter.
Snow covers my head and hides my crown...

THE SHORTENING DAYS

O the longest or the shortest day.
All our days are shortening days!
I sang my grief, I told my tale.
And what did I say?

It's a short day, a short day,
That's all I could say.
What more could I say?
All our days are shortening days!

What I tried to tell I could not say.
What I dreamt to sing I dared not say.
And what I said I would unsay.
All our days are shortening days!

Before closing his Journal, he collected his earlier poems for an appendix he called *Malunkyaputta's Posthumous Works*. These contained the message he had intended to deliver in his green youth, when he was a student at Oxford, afflicted with universal aspirations, and had met with contempt from the visiting laureates.

Great changes were looming over an overcrowded planet. The times were more and more perplexing. The approach of the millennium provoked doomsday Speculations. Malunkyaputta wrote in his Journal "*Our Program is Interrupted.*"

"It's earthquake weather again. The long-promised day is fixed in our calendar, but it's all so different from what we expected! Suddenly we must leave our televisionary set, in the middle of our favorite program; abandon our drinks, our toys and games. The apartments are vacant; our friends and lovers missing; our last important message undelivered.

"O what a surprise! To be nullified in the wink of an eye. Our shadows, printed on the wall or stamped into the pavement; cancelled yet undelivered; undelivered and for ever undeliverable! Who'll now report for whom the minutes of the Soon- To- Be- Forgotten; who'll rehearse the acts of Nebuchadnezzar? Who'll recall the last man to land on the moon?"

Ready to leave, he surveyed the scene from his cabin. When he first came to Mount Shasta, the region was a place of solitary grandeur and the Indians considered it the dwelling place of the gods. Since then, the region had been changed by real estate speculators. The green hills and valleys between Weaversville and Eureka, the roads along Mad River and Trinity Alps, were bourgeoning with busy new towns, with shopping malls and tourist camps, Chicken Parlors, Pizza Huts. The air was tainted with the stench of new garbage dumps. The countryside everywhere bore the marks of progress.

Multitudes of immigrants were entering from Asia, Africa, South America, Mexico; refugees from all parts of the world were coming in tidal waves, hungry for greener pastures. America was Everyman's Promised Land; it was becoming a strange and divided land, more and more crowded, confused, and violent.

Malunkyaputta heard militant crusaders railing from the heartland of America: "Behold the Trojan Horse in the Camp of Democracy! Traitors, disguised as patriots, are plotting to enslave Americans. The government is our secret enemy. The politicians are tools of corporations. They're scheming to dismantle the Constitution and Bill of Rights. They'd plow under the bones of the Founding Fathers. They'd becloud the land with black helicopters, legions of policemen, armies of spies, informers, tax-collectors. They'd terrorize the country with prison camps and ever-expanding jails. We must arm ourselves and fight, before we're disarmed and powerless!

"Traitors are filling the schools with false teachers who misguide a new generation. In the name of democracy, they falsify history and promote the cult of ignorance and mediocrity. They foster the breeding of defectives. They produce a confused or cynical generation, a horde with no manners, no morals, no mind; no judgment, no taste, no style. They nourish a culture of violent consumers, gullible gamblers, would-be tyrants, and future slaves."

*   *   *

Malunkyaputta tried to discern the shape of things to come. How would modern man cope with his mounting problems? The problem of surplus population; spreading poverty; the corruption of morality and culture in a democracy? On the eve of the millennium, he tried to predict the history of the future.

The first zoologist, Aristotle considered man the most inquisitive, most imitative, and perhaps the most inventive of all the animals. Survivor of the long and grim Ice Ages, evolving man was selected to endure, prevail, and multiply. And challenging the millennium, tomorrow's people would find ways of solving their problems.

Malunkyaputta could imagine some of their solutions. After exhausting their supply of oil and other fuel, they will develop solar power and capture the sun's energy. They will harness the winds on a global scale. They will bore deep tunnels through the planet and tap the heat in the volcanic core of the Earth. They will mine the oceans for new sources of fuel, food, and drugs.

To increase their mobility, they will invent teleportation: They will use instant transformers to de-materialize and re-materialize their bodies at designated places. They will travel through space-time at the speed of light. They will visit distant planets and try to colonize Mars or Pluto, though this may prove impractical and illusory.

To cope with population pressure on an overcrowded planet, molecular biologists and genetic engineers will gradually reduce the size of Homo sapiens. After mapping the human genome, they will manipulate the DNA and miniaturize man to the size of an ant. This will vastly increase man's living space and natural resources. (As the longest surviving and most successful society on Earth, the ants have prefigured a model society of the future.)

To extend his range of sports and pleasures, minimal man will develop a variety of new drugs and sex stimulants. He will explore the resources of Deep Sleep; Dream Induction; Alternate Realities. He will test the promise of Hibernation; Estivation; Cryogenics; Suspended Animation; and even Temporary Euthanasia. He may program himself to attain a state of Chronic Bliss or Perpetual Ecstasy, which may resemble the State of Nirvana...

By some such means, man might enjoy the millennium: a thousand years of Peace and Tranquility.

On the other hand, as a creature of unlimited hungers and irrational drives, man might find ways of destroying himself. It was also possible that Nature, so long disturbed and exploited, might bid him farewell. A random meteor from outer space could bombard the Earth and extinguish all life on the planet. Or a new virus, a plague more virulent than AIDS, could reduce the population to zero, the way the dinosaurs were reduced some fifty million years ago. Even more likely, a new strong man with gangs of terrorists could precipitate a nuclear holocaust. And that would put an end to the story.

In line with his ruminations, he added a fable to his Journal:

Long after a chain reaction from a nuclear holocaust had extinguished the human race, a few lower forms of life began to re-emerge: worms, maggots, snails, crabs, rats, other rodents. The survivors included a few gibbons who had found shelter on a desolate little island east of Papua.

One day an inquisitive gibbon discovered a human skull in the sand on the beach. The gibbon inspected it, then summoned his elders. They called a council and studied the skull.

"What was the meaning of man?" they wondered. "What was his purpose?"

A philosophical young gibbon proposed that they compile a brief history, *The Rise and Fall of the Manimal.* "Our descendants might learn from his mistakes." Another objected: "It cannot be done. We don't know why he acted as he did..." Still another remarked: "His history can be told in a nutshell: He came, he crowed, he polluted the Earth. He left in a hurry, in total confusion. The best part was his exit..."

The oldest gibbon remarked: "All the same, he had great gifts and mighty powers —"

The second oldest observed: "He mastered all creation —"

The youngest one added ruefully: "But the master of creation could not master himself!"

Shaking their heads, the gibbons tossed the radiant skull back into the sea and retired to ruminate on the riddle of the manimal.

* * *

Again he heard the voices of his friends from the Ganges. They now seemed to be in a snowbound camp on Mount Shasta. Curiously enough, they were removing their furry garments and exchanging them for tropical outfits as if preparing for a safari in Africa.

"Has our quester been edified?" asked Padman-Ananda.

"The Journal Keeper has chronicled his delusions," said Our Precious Lady Stepmother.

"He's furnished clues to his mystery," said Mia.

"Has he completed our experiment?" asked Padman-Ananda.

"Our poet imitates many voices," said Precious Lady Stepmother. "Reborn on the Wheel, he'd try many lives…"

"He craves to be all things to all men…" said Mia. "Bird of many feathers: Bard of Nirvana…"

"Will his edification assure his nullification?" asked Padman-Ananda.

"The prophet would probe the future and play the prognosticator," said Our Precious Lady Stepmother. "Peering into the millennium, he'd foretell the course of eternity. Yet he cannot predict his own tomorrow, nor foretell his next or last minute on earth."

"He suffers from many ailments. His hereditary complaints: a compulsive vocalizer, he remains inquisitive, imitative, irrational…"

"He suffers from his current complaints: Confusion. Depression. Self-delusion. A craving for fantasy. A hunger for the absurd. Flight from the real. The schizzy trail…"

"Progressive ignorance. Paranoia. Regression. Infinite regression…"

"Is he responsible for his ailments? He's a victim of his genetic faults. An evolutionary blunder… Who can cure him?"

"Unable to learn from the past, he may return to his beginnings…"

"Escaping the Wheel, he may become Nothing…."

Chapter XII. The Interpreter

(1)

Descending from Mount Shasta, he moved slowly down the steep and rocky trails, then ambled westward for three days, making his way through the wilderness toward the Pacific Ocean. He carried a backpack which held a supply of bread and honey and his Journal. Following Trinity River, he passed through hidden green valleys with deep gorges, gray-black boulders, and foaming white waters. South of Eureka, he reached a majestic grove of redwood trees and entered a clearing, a mysterious and primeval place called Headwaters. The higher branches of the thousand-year-old redwoods formed nesting shelters for sea birds, murrelets, great-horned owls and ravens.

In the distance, through the green mist of the grove, he could see a swarm of children. They were coming toward him, running and shouting, an endless number of many-hued children, still new to the world.

They surrounded Malunkyaputta and wanted to learn his story.

"Tell us your secret," they asked the bearded old hermit.

"I have no secrets," Malunkyaputta told them. "I search for the truth."

"Is that your secret?" they shouted.

"All my secrets are open secrets," he told them. "I speak only the truth."

"What is the truth?" asked the children.

"Truth is elusive and ever-changing," said Malunkyaputta. "Man is a riddle yet to be solved. The answers lie in man's mind perhaps."

"What is man's mind?" asked a child.

The old man explained as best he could: "Mind is a lion that roars when it's hungry. Mind is a hive of bees, overflowing with honey. Mind is a mirror, a world within a world. Mind is a key to the universe. Mind is a black hole that can never be filled…"

He tried to speak his truth but the words he used kept changing their meaning even while he was speaking, and the children didn't understand him.

"Have I mind too?" asked one.

"Everyone shares everyone's mind," said Malunkyaputta. "But each one's mind is different. The Hummingbird Mind flies in all directions. The Chameleon Mind changes every minute. The Magpie Mind steals trash and treasure. The Grasshopper Mind jumps from atoms to galaxies…"

"Tell us your story!" the children demanded.

Malunkyaputta gazed at them. He looked up at the tall trees that surrounded them and recited his tale.

(2)

"Like most of my neighbors, I was born naked, hungry, and ignorant. Naked, I was clad by others; hungry, I was nourished by others… Green in the springtime of my wayward youth, I sat by Buddha's feet and tried to fathom his meaning. Craving more edification, I asked too many questions. He called me a quibbler and 'Be a lamp unto yourself,' he said, 'or dwell in the shade of delusion.' My fellow disciple, Padman-Ananda drove me away… Now at this time I had a high ambition: I wanted to discover the real cause and cure of man's unhappiness. And I wanted to sing a new song, a song to delight all creatures, a song that had never been sung before…

"Imitating my master, I became a mendicant in Bombay. A strange old woman, whom I called My Precious Lady Step-mother, furnished me with a begging bowl. She had rescued me as an infant when I was floating down the Ganges on a tide of corpses, abortions, and other garbage. Both kind and cruel, she had saved me and fed me; she also whipped and starved me. A young woman, whom I called Mia gave me a mirror that reflected the moon and the stars and the ever-changing images of beauty. Spellbound by Mia, I pursued the beautiful. I lost myself in a maze.

"Searching for more edification, I became a wandering scholar. I learned the occult arts of Tibet. Infinitely curious, I mastered the trick of levitation and, pursuing my quest through time and space, I interviewed the wisest men of antiquity in various incarnations. At intervals I became a Hindu, an Egyptian, a Greek; a white man, a black man, a Jew. My research offended the gurus in Tibet. They charged me with vanity, self-seeking, and mindlessness. They cast me out. Bereft of my occult arts, I drifted through the snowbound Himalayas and fell into an icy crevice. Frozen solid, I suffered virtual death.

"After a deep sleep of some 2500 years, I woke up in London. Suffering a rebirth, I resumed my quest for edification. I attended the best schools in Europe, I heard the masters of science and philosophy. As always, I asked too many questions. They too called me a quibbler and dismissed me for a fool.

"Bewildered by the scholars, I visited the Holy Land, once the home of poets and prophets. Standing by the western wall in Jerusalem, I heard the lamentations of the Jews, a God-seeking remnant of tribes chosen for rejection. I roamed in the Negeb in search of light and lost myself in the desert. I nearly died of thirst by the Dead Sea. On the verge of death, I had a dream which changed my fortune.

"Following a formula from my dream, I invented a faucet, a faucet with a filter that converted salt water into sweet water, and the water would raise new crops to feed the hungry. I patented my invention and became immensely rich. For a time, I indulged in my pleasures from the world's supply of goods and evil. But my pleasures did not satisfy me.

"On my 30th birthday, I remembered the poor and felt a new surge of pity for them. I wanted to cure their unhappiness. I gave away my riches and became a teacher of the people. I preached them the gospel of science, the way of reason.

'I bring you good news,' I told them. 'News of a new Eden for all men to share.'

'You speak of strange things,' they said. 'Why should we believe you?'

'I speak the truth,' I said. 'I want to help you —'

'You gave away your riches. So how can you help us?'

'I'm a citizen of one world,' I told them. 'The Earth's my home, it belongs to all, and all men are my brothers. This is true for you as well as for me.'

'You're homeless and hungry,' they taunted me. 'Poor among the poor, with nothing but words to share. And no man calls you his brother. Young and mad from spring to winter, old and mad all your days, you will live and die a stranger among strangers. At the end you'll jump into your crematorium as if escaping from your long exile in the realm of delusion!'

"So the poor rejected my lesson. When I preached from Mount Palomar and warned them of a day of reckoning, they called me a false prophet and tried to kill me. They cast me into a pit. I barely escaped. They vowed to catch me; sooner or later, they'd tear me to pieces.

"I fled into the wilderness and built myself a shelter on Mount Shasta. I despised the stupid tribe of breeders. I wanted to secede from the human race.

"So I grew old in the woods. I sang wild songs to amuse myself. I played the clown. I logged my perishing days and nights in my book of withering minutes, to tell my story: it has turned into a Dream Book."

Malunkyaputta smiled at the children.

"So I've come to the end of my story," he said. "I've told you as much as I can... You see before you a bearded old boy at the end of his quest, short of breath and shorn of his vanities. I'd sing a new song for you, but my voice is gone; I'd dance a new dance, but my bones are brittle. Adieu, children of time. I leave you in the forest..."

The children did not understand him. They babbled nonsense rhymes as he turned to leave them:

> Ma-lunk-lunk-lunk
> Plink-plank-plunk
> Chimp-champ-chump
> Ma-ma, Da-da, Ba-ba, Ka-ka
> Plink-plank-plunk

Now a new multitude of strange children swarmed into the clearing and surrounded Malunkyaputta.

They were fuzzy little creatures with bright wild eyes, sharp teeth, and clawlike hands coated with soft brown fur. They were gurgling, chuckling, chortling or yelping; they made barking sounds as if trying to imitate human speech. They were vocalizing in chimp-chant or screaming in chimpish.

And now he saw, as in a flash of lightning, the answer to the riddle that had tormented him. The children were devolving! Nature had reversed the course of evolution. Homo sapiens was returning to his roots, resuming his links with his ancestral tribe of apes: the chimpanzees, gorillas, orangutans; the gibbons and baboons, among other missing links. All the clues pointed in this direction. The evidence was unmistakable!

Devolution was the explanation.

Malunkyaputta felt a surge of triumph for a few moments. At last he had penetrated the mystery. O what a revelation! What a stupefying discovery! Greater than Newton's gravity, better than Darwin's hypothesis, deeper than Einstein's relativity! He rejoiced in his illumination with increasing grandiosity.

His breakthrough marked a turning point in the history of science. His theory superseded Darwin's theory. The descent of man was checked by the ascent of the ape. Man's so-called progress toward perfection had camouflaged his regress: his increasing confusion, violence, and bestiality. The survival of the fittest had developed into the survival of the most aggressive and greediest, morally the most defective.

Malunkyaputta now saw the truth, or so he thought. He had reached the last step in his quest for edification. Looking back at his adventures as a missionary, he now saw his fellows from a new perspective. As ever, they were chittering, gibbering, howling, strutting, noise-making creatures; stalking, snaring or sneering, imitating each other; cheating, deceiving, enslaving, exploiting; perpetually in heat, lusting and copulating; battering, beating, or killing each other. He saw them in their simian aspect. The change had been gradual and their enormous vanity blinded them to their condition. Pretending to be human, they were in fact unhappy apes. Rather than made in the image of God, man was a mutant beast.

Rather than godlike, he was a disturbed and disturbing creature, a menace to the earth and to the more innocent animals in the kingdom of God. The paragon was nature's freak and monsterpiece; a moon-walking anomaly; an absurdity.

Malunkyaputta's theory explained the causes of man's suffering and unhappiness. Over-breeding led to hunger, pollution, hostility, and ever more destructive violence. It endangered the whole planet. Now nature was trying to restore the broken balance. As the whales and dolphins had returned to their earlier home the sea, so man was returning to his simian home the jungle. Simian regression was nature's safety-valve; an effort to save the Earth from man's irrational destructiveness.

* * *

Malunkyaputta had forsaken his gospel of science. Despite their superior craft, scientists often resembled the terrorists; they furnished weapons of mass murder to their masters. In the 20th century, modern man had killed more than 100 million of his fellowmen. The record was the most dismal in man's history. Once the primitive hunter, modern man was becoming a paranoid ape. The evidence was overwhelming. Pursuing his urge to kill and to multiply, Homo sapiens had triggered nature's response... Malunkyaputta had once aspired to become a universal poet, with a hopeful message for mankind. His quest for edification had led to his last discovery: Simian regression. This indeed was a universal message.

He himself was regressing, he knew. Emulating the sages, he had failed to recognize his own apish craving for mimicry. He had imitated Buddha, Socrates, Paul, Zarathustra. Even now, at the end of his quest, with his Theory of Devolution he was imitating Darwin. Was this then his last lesson in self-edification? His thoughts were becoming less and less coherent. He caught a glimpse of himself as a white-bearded ape in a preposterous opera vocalizing his farewell aria to an empty house...

* * *

Was his theory true or false or merely preposterous?

He reviewed his case and tried to piece together once again the clues, the symptoms, the ever-multiplying facts which pointed to simian regression. Could he doubt the evidence? After all, more than 90 per cent of his genes were the same as the chimpanzee's. A late link in nature's chain of experiments, Homo sapiens was no doubt an unstable animal, afflicted with apish drives and godlike aspirations. Confounded by his strange gift of reason, he'd pursue the Good, the True, and the Beautiful, yet produced an ever-mounting heap of planetary Misery, Falsehood, and Ugliness.

A singing or shrieking ape. A singularity. Time's monsterpiece. A moon-walking anomaly. An absurdity. O what a paradox! Imitator, mimic, pretender, impersonator, he was forever poking, probing, pecking, picking, penetrating. Wit-picker, nit-picker, flea-hunter. Quintessential quibbler. An anthropoid ape with delusions of grandeur.

He saw three old friends from the Ganges, with their legendary robes and godlike features, revealed in a simian light.

"Observe the priest," he told himself, "speculating on heaven and hell. The philosopher, probing the mind. The scientist, peering into matter; the statesman, promoting his program; the poet, pursuing his fantasy; the general, plotting his strategy. And see the inquisitive ape, opening Pandora's Box. See the lustful ape, breeding new swarms for starvation! See the violent ape and see the tormented and tormenting ape-man, struggling to break his bars!

"Mongrel of mongrels, I may call myself what I will; heir of the ages; master of the planet; fittest of fit; prophet, messiah, universal bard — I remain a brother of the chimpanzees!"

His theory of devolution explained his own peculiar history and the human condition. Yet much remained a mystery. After all, the progeny of apes had produced not only a Nero, Stalin, Hitler. It had produced a Plato, a Shakespeare, a Bach. Scores of questers had emerged from the human jungle. A Jefferson, a Lincoln, an Einstein. Some had walked on the moon; others had aspired to visit the stars... Despite his flaws and limitations, Homo sapiens had been a remarkable experiment.

Epilogue: The Self-Edifier

Malunkyaputta wandered off alone, moving deeper into the forest. A spring wind rose from the Pacific and blew through the redwood grove. He dropped his backpack on the loam, then flung his Journal into the wind. Like a cloud of white birds, the scattered pages flew into the air.

> What is the wind?
> What is the wind trying to sing?
> The wind blows where it will.
> Who can tell the wind anything?

He seemed to be flying toward the stars, as if practicing his old skill in levitation, like one of Chagall's wonder-working rabbis. At the same time, his body lay flat on the ground like a bundle of dry sticks.

Lying on the loam of the redwood grove, he was preparing to rejoin the earth. His shrunken body, his meagre dark face, half-hidden by strands of wild white hair, suggested a forest creature.

In the dimming green light of the afternoon, he was alone as always, yet a part of the earth and sky, the clouds and the shadows of clouds. He was a part of all that he had known. A deep silence was entering him, yet a silence full of faint voices. A few small birds flew in and out of the trees; a few wild deer stepped into the clearing to gaze at him. He could hear an owl calling from a distance, an owl hidden in a tall tree calling to her mate: the sweetest sound he had ever heard.

He was beginning to hear and see as never before. He could hear the grass grow. He could hear invisible legions of tiny ants tunnelling the earth under the grass. He could hear the soughing wind as it moved in the trees humming its eternal Aum. He could see prisms of light in a dew-drop, shimmering in rainbow colors. In the stream of light he could feel the gyrations of protons and electrons in the perpetual dance of the elements. For a moment he could feel the pulse that linked him to the volcanic heart of the earth and to receding galaxies aeons away. Every cell in his body was composed of star dust: for a moment at least, he could oscillate between the earth and the stars.

Was he dreaming, awakening, or falling asleep for ever? "What am I?" he wondered. He was beginning to see the unfathomable strangeness of the real. "How beautiful the earth," he whispered to himself, "that drew us out of molten rock and thundercloud! How beautiful its ever-flowing waters, its many curious creatures…"

The random particles of light seemed to be singing in many voices. Was this the music of the Spheres? The music of Silence? The voice of God? Or the sound of an alien force, an incomprehend-god perhaps, infinite in fantasy and invention and for ever improvising?

Again he was asking questions without an answer. Again he was a young quibbler in the deer park by the Ganges.

(2)

Buddha was smiling at him from the trunk of a redwood tree, which resembled the familiar bodhi tree of enlightenment.

Malunkyaputta rose and approached his old teacher who greeted him serenely.

"Well, Malunkyaputta. Have you been edified?" Buddha spoke as if their ancient conversation had but recently been interrupted.

"I asked too many questions," said Malunkyaputta. "Questions without an answer."

"What did I tell you?" asked the Buddha.

"You taught me Alpha and Omega, without the abracadabra. You taught me the cause of suffering. You showed me the way to Nirvana. But I needed to know more."

"Yes, you searched far, indeed. And what did you learn?"

"I moved from illusion to illusion; I lost myself in a maze of mysteries. I called my old riddles new revelations. I deceived myself—"

"I know, my friend. That's every poet's problem."

"You taught the truth, as best you could. Desire's the cause of man's suffering. Yet in spite of your teaching, people have kept multiplying."

"Yes. That is their habit."

"Too many breeders," said Malunkyaputta. "Now more than ever before. The majority, born to suffer. What's to be done? I tried to teach them, the best I could. They would not believe me. They remain the children of chaos. And as long as men and women lust for each other, they will breed and multiply and overcrowd the earth. Overcrowding is the cause of hunger, hatred, and war. People devour the earth, then devour each other. Nothing can stop them. The old wheel of suffering turns and turns to grind down new generations like Vishnu's terrible wagon, the Juggernaut! What could I do?"

Buddha smiled serenely.

"Be a lamp unto yourself," he repeated. "And let your light shine like the silent stars. Abandon your little self for the universal self—"

"I have nothing but my little self," said Malunkyaputta. "And even that seems now an illusion—"

"I know, I know," said Buddha. "It's the same with me. But we should keep our littleness a secret, shouldn't we? Or they may try to cage us."

Buddha laughed at his joke, then embraced Malunkyaputta and whispered in his ear: "You are my disciple, old boy, in spite of yourself, O Venerable Malunkyaputta ..."

His smiling image faded into a tree trunk and Malunkyaputta was lying on the loam as before, curled in a fetal position.

(3)

A helicopter landed on the clearing and Malunkyaputta saw his three old friends emerging from the cockpit below the whirring blades. They wore splendid white hunting outfits as if returning from a long and successful safari. They approached him with beaming faces, gathering small fallen branches on the way.

"Congratulations!" said Padman-Ananda. "You have reconciled with the Buddha. Free from conceit, you found your way to enlightenment."

"Rejoice in your bliss!" cried Our Precious Lady Stepmother. "You know your karma. You've completed our experiment. You'll not be born again!"

"Good Morning, Malunkyaputta!" sang Mia. "You've awakened at last. You understand your nothingness. You're nearing Nirvana…"

Smiling at him, they heaped the dry branches around him, then lit the pyre.

While the flames were consuming his body, they sang their parting song in voices that merged with a faint unearthly music:

> Farewell, Awakened One.
> Awakened from a bed of shadows,
> Awakened from a realm of sorrow,
> Awakened from a prison of dreams...
>
> Free from the Wheel, turning and returning.
> The Wheel of Pain and Pleasure,
> The Wheel of Time, the Self, the Mind and Memory,
> The Wheel of Illusion
>
> Fly, O Bird of Fire!
> Fly on your wings of flame.
> Fly from the Cage of Desire,
> Fly from the Snare of Delusion,
> Fly from the Here and the Now,
> Fly to the Everlasting…
> *Mantra, tantra, dharma, karma….*

So they sang. And even as they sang, their white garments turned into the dark dust-colored robes of forgotten household gods, and his timeless friends faded from the clearing. In a little while Malunkyaputta himself became a drift of smoke that rose toward the sky to rejoin an unpredictable universe.

www.ingramcontent.com/pod-product-compliance
Lightning Source LLC
Chambersburg PA
CBHW030634130626
46552CB00002B/840